Red Rock Canyon
The Apache Warrior
A Tyrell Sloan western adventure

Written by Brian T. Seifrit

Email: **briantseifrit@gmail.com**

Web site: www.booksbybriant.ca

Cover art by: Getty Creations, Burnaby, British Columbia

The Apache Warrior
A Tyrell Sloan western adventure

Published by

ISBN: 978-1-9992595-9-4 Paperback
ISBN: 978-1-990215-13-1 Hardcover
ISBN: 978-1-7773169-0-7 eBook

Copyright Brian T. Seifrit © June 2019

The Apache Warrior
A Tyrell Sloan western adventure

Chapter 1

On December 20, 1891, Tyrell Sloan *aka* Travis Sweet, Riley Scott, and Colby Christian, along with Black Dog, left behind those staying at Pete Cross's place, and headed into uncharted Indian Territory, in search of the Apache Kid. The Athabasca warrior known as Crying Wolf travelled with them for a distance.

"We have traveled now for three days, together. It is here that I turn north and return to my people. I will not forget these past months. I can now return knowing I have avenged my brother and niece's deaths."

Crying Wolf looked northwardly.

"You, Travis, and your friends will have a long journey ahead of you. I know who it is now that you seek. He is the squared jaw Apache. Although the Apache are brothers of ours, who left our lands to travel far and wide, he is no friend of the Athabasca," Crying Wolf lied. "But heed my warning. There are few from other tribes that will protect him. Those ones will be found on the southern plains."

Crying Wolf reached into his quiver of depleted arrows and handed one to Tyrell.

"As always, this arrow will protect you in the northern regions where the Athabasca call home, take it."

Tyrell reached over and took the arrow.

"I thank you for your friendship Crying Wolf. If I had something, I could hand off to you as we part ways I would. Instead I leave you with respect and gratitude, of which you'll always have from me," Tyrell stuck the arrow into his rolled up bedroll.

"And for you, young Colby," Crying Wolf began as he reached into his waistband and withdrew his .45 Colt Ranger. "You need practice with this, take it; I do not want it anymore."

"What do you mean? I got my rifle Crying Wolf," Colby pointed out.

"Yes, but not always will a long gun be of use. This you will learn as time goes by."

"Well, Jesus, I don't know what to offer back."

"Nothing, this is not a trade. I want you to have this pistol."

Colby inhaled deeply and took the offering along with a handful of bullets. He looked the pistol over and nodded.

"I ain't used one of these but on a few occasions, it looks like a mighty fine pistol. I do thank you for it Crying Wolf."

"It is a means of both safety and my apologies to you for when I took your horse," Crying Wolf and the others chuckled.

"Uh-huh, well then, I guess I'll accept it," Colby smiled back as he tucked it into his belt and put the handful of bullets into his front jacket pocket.

Crying Wolf now looked at Riley.

"For you Riley, I have no parting gift except for our continued friendship past and present."

"And as always Crying Wolf, you have mine," Riley smiled and nodded.

Crying Wolf leaned forward on his horse and looked at the three riders individually.

"The next time we may meet might be long in coming or may never come to fruition. Remember this for if and when such a time comes, the Athabasca are at peace with you."

Then wishing them luck one last time he headed north.

"You take care of that wound Crying Wolf, and you can bet that we'll meet again," Tyrell said as the three of them watched him head into the northern horizon. That was December 23, 1891. For a brief moment in time, the three riders continued their gaze as the silhouette of their friend Crying Wolf faded into the shadows of that warm December day.

Turning their own horses now, they headed southwest toward the township of Falkland, a small mining town that they had all agreed to begin their search for the Apache Kid. It was also a place Riley knew had a telegraph office. It wasn't a big town by any means. It was big enough however that hoodwinks and the like were often found there, due to the turnover rate of mineworkers. It was a good place to launch their search.

"Colby, you were mentioning back at Cross's place, that you knew a little about the Apache Kid. Since we haven't much spoken about it since, what can you tell me and Riley?" Tyrell questioned as to break the boredom as the three of them continued on.

Colby looked at Tyrell, "I only ever met him once. I knew his name to be Ski-be-nan-ted, which I think means Apache Kid. Anyway, Atalmore filled me in about him afterward. He'd be about thirty or thirty-one by now, I suspect. I know the Chief of the Army Scouts adopted him back in eighteen sixty or there about. I know later on that he enlisted with the U.S Cavalry back in the eighteen eighties, some kind of program or another that General Cook, whoever the hell that is; was putting together to help against the Apache raids, something like that anyway. He may have even been involved in the surrender of that Geronimo fellow. Also he's a damn good shot with that old .50 caliber Hawken he packs around," Colby shrugged.

"That right there is quite a bit of knowledge you have," Riley pointed out. "I've read up on him a wee bit, but I have often heard about him. Never thought, he'd head up into Canada though, it is between our borders and the U.S. borders where a lot of the hearsay and such about him is lost. I do know that he was indeed in on the pursuit of

Geronimo, back in eighteen- eighty two and eighty six, after that part of what I know, there ain't much else."

Tyrell looked at the two of them, and shook his head. He had hoped that either Riley, or Colby, had a bit more information regarding the Kid. What they knew wasn't much, but it was more than he knew.

"That is it? That is all either of you know about him?"

"Not exactly, I know also that he wasn't guilty of those first charges, or, well, leastwise that is what Atalmore told me. I think that killing came about after he found his father dead, or something," Colby once more shrugged as he paused and related back to how he felt when his own family was murdered. He knew the feeling of revenge that burned in his own soul for all those years. It couldn't have been any different, he knew, for the Apache Kid.

"But, he did kill a sheriff and a deputy, when he escaped."

"To be clear, this is all we know, is that he escaped while being transported to the Yuma Prison. Killed a sheriff and a deputy, and hasn't been found since?"

"That is about it," Riley responded as the riders grew silent and contemplated the little they knew about the man they were required to bring in.

"Not even Ed, has any other information?" Tyrell asked.

"When, I headed this way with Bash and Cannon, he was working on getting more information, was promised that some was on its way. Nothing made it to the Fort before I left though. Once we get to Falkland, we'll spend a night or two, and send wire to Ed, see if he has anything that has made its way to McCoy's yet."

"Falkland is still about four days ride ahead. By the time we get there we'll almost be looking at a new year," Tyrell commented.

"Good, means we'll have missed all the festivities of Christmas too, that don't hurt my feelings one damned bit. Never really did have much use for that holiday."

"What's a matter with Christmas?" Riley asked with a bit of a frown. He had always enjoyed it, in fact most did. He was curious to know why Colby didn't.

"Like I mentioned, I haven't much use for it. Sure, the food is good, when one has it. When one don't, it don't matter none. The only thing I ever recall about Christmas is my old man getting drunk and fighting with his family. Ma, never cared much about it either, always said the presents and such, isn't as important as simply being together with family. That though ain't always true," Colby grew silent for a short while as they continued. "I grew up not caring much about it," that was all he wanted to say about it.

"I don't care much about it either, to be honest. My old man used to drink a lot too at Christmas, I don't think he had a clear head the entire time," Tyrell chuckled.

Travelling now in silence the three riders carried onward.

Back at the Fort, Brady McCoy was at the telegraph office, he finally had a wire from Matt Crawford. He read the short note. It simply stated that Matt had made the distance to Silverton, an old mining town, and was going to spend a night there and continue onward to Whiskey Tooth George's hideaway.

Brady folded the piece of paper up and had the telegrapher send a reply. In the reply, he told Matt to head into the Yukon to a town called Mistyvale, and to look up a fellow by the name of Buck Ainsworth, whose family owned a hotel. He briefly explained why, knowing Matt would get the gist of it. There was no reason to explain more, Buck would fill him in with the details he knew once Matt made the distance.

Looking the reply over, he handed it back to the clerk, paid the fee, and proceeded back to McCoy's office. Brady was surprised actually, that Matt had made it that far in the short time that he had been travelling. Finally, arriving at the McCoy's office, he tethered his horse to the horse pole, and proceeded through the front door.

"Got a wire, from Matt, he's made it to Silverton," he announced as he tossed the folded piece of paper onto the front counter. Ed made his way over and read the telegraph himself.

"Did you send him a reply, Brady, telling him to head into the Yukon?" Ed asked as he read the telegraph again.

"Yes sir, I did. I told him to look up Buck once he gets there."

"Did you tell him why?"

"Gave him a bit of the heads up, didn't want to write it out in detail. Buck, will fill him in on the what for, and whys'," Brady turned and walked into the backroom and poured himself a coffee.

Ed followed behind.

"It is good to know at least that Matt is still alive. I honestly thought since he headed into the Athabasca that he'd have ran into trouble of some sort," Ed pulled up to the table and sat down.

"You honestly thought something was going to happen to him old man? Shit, Matt knows his ins and outs. I don't reckon he's one to be caught up in something that he can't get out of, besides, he knows that area well," Brady, pointed out as he leaned against the counter with coffee in hand.

"That don't stop shit, from happening, Brady. Anything can happen at any time, no matter how well we know or don't know something," Ed fiddled with his empty cup.

Brady taking notice of what seemed to be distraught looked at Ed solemnly.

"What's going on old man? I've noticed over the last couple days you ain't been your usual self."

"What do you mean, Brady? I'm fine."

Brady shook his head.

"Nope, I don't think so. Something is going on that you ain't telling me about. So, spit it out old man."

The room grew silent for a few minutes and Brady took a swig from his coffee.

"Well, I'm waiting, what the hell is going on?"

Ed looked over to Brady and nodded.

"There is something going on, ain't sure now is the time to mention it though."

"Bullshit, to that, the way you have been moping 'round here lately. Tells me, you have something you want to get off your chest. Keeping shit bundled up ain't going to help your old ticker," Brady smiled.

"All right, I guess I'll tell you."

Ed stood up, poured himself a coffee, and then sat back down. He gestured to Brady to sit, and waited until he did so.

"Are you comfortable, Brady?"

"Am so."

Ed sighed and looked across the table.

"Come January, I'm going to retire from this business, which puts you in charge."

"Jesus Christ old man, all I got to say about that is; it is about damn time. You've been dodging bullets long enough, and the older you get the slower you get. One day one of them bullets just might find its mark. You stepping down from this business is the best thing, that you could possibly do, while you still have all your faculties in order," Brady responded with sincerity and a smirk.

"I ain't that old Brady. I just can't keep up with it all anymore. I'm tired."

"You are tired, 'cause you are putting on the years. What does ma, say about this?"

Ed brought his cup to his lips and took a swallow.

"I ain't mentioned it to her yet. You're the only one that I've told. And until I make it official, I don't want you blabbing it."

Brady chuckled.

"I ain't going to say a word, old man. It ain't my place to say a damn thing. You ain't got to worry about that."

"Good. You know things will change once I make the announcement. I ain't sure how Riley is going to take it. He might retire himself."

"He might, and I wouldn't complain about that none either. You're both old and getting slow."

"Jesus, Brady, I would have thought you'd be a bit more concerned about how the business will run without him," Ed pointed out.

"The business won't change any, old man. The rest of us will still do what it is we do now. We got a crew of some of the best men 'round. Tanner, Matt, Travis, they're all good at what they do. They know the ins and outs of this business. We'd be less two men that is all. Nothing else would change. Besides, if it was warranted, we could always hire a couple of new men."

"You can't just hire new men, Brady. You'd have to hire men that have been in the business. Men that know the risks involved."

"No. Really old man, I was thinking if we needed I'd hire a couple of men from the saloon," Brady joked.

"Go ahead and make jokes all you want Brady, but hiring for this type of business isn't easy. You have to trust those you hire with your life. They have to know how to shoot and handle themselves in perilous conditions. There aren't many men around like that anymore."

"That is because we already have them on our payroll," Brady smiled.

"Well, I won't deny that. We do have a hell of a crew, don't we?"

"That we do. Trust me old man, I wouldn't hire anyone that I didn't feel couldn't handle the job. Hell, with the crew we already have, I don't see any reason right now to even worry about looking for more men. I'm comfortable with the ones we have. There ain't anything our crew and I couldn't do," Brady made clear as he took the last swig from his coffee.

Sliding his chair out from the table, he stood up and put his empty cup into the sink.

"I'm glad we had this talk old man, I knew something was eating at you."

Ed nodded.

"I'll admit the thought of me retiring was eating at me. Wasn't sure I was being honest with myself, and I was second guessing the decision to do so. I ain't second-guessing myself anymore. Come January, I will retire."

"All right, so now that we have that out of the way, I guess we can carry on with what this day is going to bring."

Exiting the backroom, Brady made his way over to his desk and sat down to a pile of paperwork, and he started thumbing through it all. His mind though wasn't on the work at hand and for a few minutes, he reminisced. He had always known that Ed would eventually retire and that he'd be the one running McCoy's.

However as he sat there, he wondered if he was indeed up to the task. There was a lot to running the business and although he had been taught by Ed over the years on how to do it. He wasn't sure he had the skills. What he had to do was accept the fact that soon enough, it would all be up to him on how McCoy's would continue to grow.

Chapter 2

On December 24 after four days of heavy riding, Tyrell, Riley, Colby and Black Dog, finally made the distance to Falkland. Not surprisingly, wreaths hung on street posts, and from the windows and doors of residences and shops. Pulling up to the horse pole outside the Falkland Hotel, the three men dismounted and looked around.

"Seems pretty merry around here, don't it," Colby said with little enthusiasm as he tethered his horse.

"It is Christmas, Colby. I hope we can get us a hotel room that is all I care about at the present," Riley chuckled, "see what I did there- *present*."

Tyrell smiled and shook his head.

"Nice play on words, Riley."

Colby stood there numb.

"Let me add this, there ain't no time like the present, to find out if we can get rooms. So, let's get to it," Colby turned and made his way to the entrance. He looked back to the others, who were looking around at all the decorations that lit up the small town.

"You two care to get a room or what?"

"Sheesh, right behind you Colby, c'mon Riley, the kid is going to wet himself if we don't follow. Black Dog you stay near and keep the horses in check."

Tyrell and Riley made their way over to Colby. Entering they approached the front counter and rang the bell. A couple minutes later, a young woman came out from a backroom.

"Good evening. Are the three of you here for rooms?" she asked.

Colby taken back by her beauty fumbled with his hat as Tyrell answered her.

"Yes, ma'am, three singles if possible, or a double, and a single. Whatever is available I reckon."

The young woman looked through a book on the counter.

"We do have two doubles available, but no single rooms. Would two doubles be all right?"

Tyrell looked back at Riley and Colby.

"There are a couple of doubles available, is that all right with you two? We'll flip a coin later to see who bunks with whom and who gets to sleep alone."

Tyrell chuckled, as he looked back at the young woman.

"Yeah, two doubles will have to do. Is there a chance we can get baths added to the cost? We've been on the trail a few days."

"We can have baths set up, yes. The cost for the two rooms and three baths will be eight dollars per night for the rooms, and one dollar for each of the baths. How long do you plan on staying?"

Tyrell scratched his head as he looked back to the others. "How long do you reckon we should stay?" he asked them.

"Two days at least, I'd think," Riley responded.

Tyrell nodded, "All right, I guess we'll book the rooms for two days," he reached into his pocket and fished out a few bucks, counting off what he needed he handed the money over. In turn, she smiled and handed him two keys.

"Rooms six and nine," she said, "your baths will be ready in about an hour. The bathing room is on the second floor too, so you aren't very far from it."

"Thank you," Tyrell said as he and the others turned heel and headed to their rooms.

"So, who gets what?" Colby asked as they climbed the stairs.

"I don't mind bunking with you Colby," Riley joked. He had seen the look on Colby's face when the young woman and he locked eyes. Riley might be old but he was no fool.

"Shit, I was hoping to bunk with Colby, so I didn't have to listen to that God awful snoring of yours, Riley," Tyrell added to the mix.

Colby stood there looking at both of them. He wasn't sure they were serious or not, or if they were both blind. Hadn't they seen the look he and the young woman shared? He didn't want to bunk with either of them. He wanted a room all to himself, for obvious reasons.

Tyrell and Riley both noting Colby's apprehension, began to chuckle.

"No worries, Colby. You go ahead and take room nine," Tyrell tossed him the key.

"Jesus, I thought you two were serious and that one of yous was going to bunk with me."

"We ain't blind Colby. We were funning with you. We saw how you and that young woman looked at each other. Take my advice though, at the *present*," Tyrell chuckled. "You need to clean yourself up, before talking to a beautiful maiden such as that young lady downstairs. You stink, plain and simple."

"You and Riley ain't no bed of roses either there Travis. So, *presently* you can stick that up your ass," Colby now chuckled as he turned and made his way to room nine.

Tyrell and Riley watched as he traipsed onward to a room all of his own.

"You want to make a wager that he gets slapped and not slippery," Riley, joked, as Tyrell unlocked the door to the room, they were going to share.

"I don't know, Riley, I think the kid has a chance. He and that young woman never took their eyes off one another. Colby was dumbfounded. I thought for sure you were going to have to lift his jaw up off the ground."

"Hell no, I was waiting for his tongue to hit the floor, so I could have wiped my boots off."

The two of them laughed as they looked around their room.

"Not a bad looking room. The beds look cozy enough," Tyrell sat down at the foot of one of them, and bounced up and down. "I'm going to sleep like a baby tonight."

Riley made his way over to the other bed, and tossed his gear onto it.

"I hope there is a telegraph office around, we need to get word to Ed that we're on the move, and wait to see if he has anything more to share on the Apache Kid,"

Riley now sat down.

"Or we'll be going after him blind, and I hate having to do shit that way. Best to know everything there is to know, then to know nothing at all."

Tyrell fell back onto the bed and pushed his hat over his eyes.

"You know what Riley," he began as he inhaled deeply. "Right as you are, that it is best to know, as much as we can about that Apache Kid. I'd say we are days away from making any headway into that affair. I want nothing more than to simply relax for a day or two…" that was all he said before he was soon snoring.

Riley shook his head.

"Well, you go ahead and rest up princess. I'll go look for a telegraph office."

Standing, Riley exited the room and made his way outside. He looked up and down the street and finally spotting the Post Office, he walked the distance. From there he could get directions on where the telegraph office was, if it wasn't in the same building.

Entering he wiped his boots off on the entrance rug and walked up to the counter.

"Is there a telegraph office around here?" he asked the clerk who met him at the counter.

"Yes sir. Right here, where do you want to send a wire?" the clerk asked as he picked up a pencil and piece of paper and handed it to Riley.

"To Fort MacLeod," Riley said as he took the pencil and jaunted down a few words. He handed the piece of paper back. The clerk looked it over and tapped out the message.

"There all sent," he said as he handed the original message back. "That'll be seventy-five cents."

Riley pulled out a few coins and handed them to the clerk.

"Any chance I can be notified if something comes back in the next hour or so? I'm staying at the Falkland Hotel. The name is Riley."

"Sure, if something comes back before we close for the holiday, I'll make sure you get notified. You said your name is Riley?"

"That is right, Riley Scott, and I'm staying at the hotel down the street."

"Good enough. Thank you Mr. Scott," the clerk said as he tossed Riley's payment into a drawer.

Riley nodded his thanks and headed back the way he had come. Not wanting to disturb Tyrell's rest he ventured to the saloon and ordered a whisky as he sat at the long bar. He swiveled around to look over the small crowd of town folk that were partaking in a few joyful Christmas Eve drinks.

Everything was as it should be, folks having a good time and making small talk on what they hoped, for the New Year. He smiled to himself as he downed his second whisky. His hope for the New Year was that he lived through it.

Standing now, he made his way up the stairs and to his shared room. Tyrell by now was awake and was picking through his gear fetching cleaner clothes and what not.

"Hey, Riley, where did you get to?" Tyrell asked.

"Got a wire sent off to Ed, and had a couple shots of whisky down at the saloon. I take it the baths is ready?"

"Yep, was told so not more than a couple minutes ago, there is only one bath though and I ain't willing to jump into the sudsy water with you. So, you want to take the first one or what?"

"Nah, you go ahead. I think it is my turn to rest my eyes," Riley sprawled out on his bed and tilted his hat over his face.

"All right, well, when I get done I'll let you know."

Tyrell grabbed his gear and headed to the bathing area, he was met half way by Colby.

"Are you heading to the bath, Travis?" Colby asked.

"I was, you going that way too?"

"Was so."

"All right well, you go ahead. I'll take the next."

"Are you sure?"

"Am so, go ahead Colby, you stink worse than me anyway," Tyrell smiled. "I'll check up on the horses and Black Dog. You don't mind dropping these off do you?" he asked referring to his clean clothes and razor.

"Sure, should I toss them on the dirty floor?" Colby teased.

"Don't do that, they're the last clean clothes I got," Tyrell handed the gear over.

"No worries," Colby said as he took Tyrell's gear and continued on his way to the bath.

Tyrell turned around and headed outside. To his surprise, Black Dog wasn't in sight. He looked around until finally spotting him down at a butcher shop gnawing on a bone. He shook his head and chuckled, as he made his way over to where Black Dog sat.

"It didn't take you long to make a friend I see. That is one hell of a big bone Black Dog."

Tyrell knelt next to him and patted him.

"How did you mange to con a butcher out of that?"

Black Dog looked up to him and panted then continued gnawing his bone. The door to the butcher shop opened and out stepped a man.

"Is that your dog, mister?" the man asked.

"He is. Do I owe you for the bone?"

"Not at all, I thought the dog was a stray and he looked hungry, so I gave him the bone. He is a mighty fine looking dog. What is his name?"

Tyrell stood up from his crouching stance and smiled.

"I call him Black Dog and I thank you for giving him that bone. It'll keep him busy for the next couple of days while I'm in town."

"Are you going to join in with the festivities tomorrow then?"

"I ain't sure about that," Tyrell answered.

"Oh, geez, the town puts on quite the shin-ding, on Christmas day. Music, dancing, sleigh rides for the young and old, folks from all around show up. Church services go on all day. It is quite a good time, you should join us."

"Well, sir, I thank you for the invite. You never know, I might see you. By the way, can you point me to the livery? I have three horses that need feeding and to be stabled."

"Sure can, you'll find the livery stable up behind the Post Office."

The man pointed.

"All right, well thank you very much mister," Tyrell said as he tilted his hat in appreciation. "C'mon Black Dog, let's get."

Black Dog snaffled up the bone and trailing close behind Tyrell, he followed. A short while later with the horses stabled and permission given to allow Black Dog to stay at the stable too, Tyrell headed back to the hotel, and the hot bath he had been longing for all day.

There was a message stuck in a little box that was fastened to the door, and he removed it as he unlocked the door and stepped in. Riley was snoring so loudly that the widows seemed to rattle. Tyrell, slapped at Riley's feet as he walked by.

"Wake up, Riley. Got a message here from the Fort," Tyrell said as he sat down on one of the chairs. Riley stirred and then sat up.

"Yeah, what does the message say?" he asked.

"Says, 'message received, nothing new to report on AK', which I assume is the Apache Kid," Tyrell said as Riley rubbed his eyes.

"Damn it! I was hoping for something more substantial than that."

Riley stood up and stretched.

"You know what that means, Travis?"

"Means Ed ain't got nothing more to share, which in turn means we ain't got nothing new to go on, or where to even start looking," Tyrell sighed. "It is all part of this damn job ain't it Riley."

"I'm afraid so. What I know is that the Apache Kid and those running with him like to rustle cattle.

I guess that is where we start. We can find out if anything like that has been going on around here, and then we go from there I guess. The Mounties would be informed about such things, but I'll be damned if I know where the nearest Mounted Police station is. I know Falkland ain't got one," Riley commented.

"I'm sure someone would point us in the direction of the nearest station. However, I ain't going to be asking anybody about that tonight. No sir, I'm taking a bath, having a shave and eating some food. We'll start this charade off in the morning," Tyrell replied as he headed for his long awaited bath.

By 7:00 pm that evening all three men were cleaned, shaved, and were now sitting down at the saloon, a jug of draft sat in the middle of the table and a bottle of house whisky close by. Their empty dinner plates had been taken away already, and now they were enjoying a few drinks and mild conversation.

Sometime later Colby vanished, both Tyrell and Riley knew where he had got to, and so they headed upstairs to their shared room. It didn't take long for either of them to fall asleep. Colby on the other hand slept little that night, the young woman they met earlier that day at the front counter was named Victoria and her and Colby had slipped away to his room, where a night of unmentionables took place.

Chapter 3

Christmas day, 1891, was uneventful for the three men, and on December 27, after receiving another wire from the Fort that Ed sent, they were once more on the move.

The wire was basic with little to no new information regarding the Apache Kid, or those that rode with him. What it did contain and was as important was that Barclay Atalmore and his Rebel Ranger's had been identified and spotted south-west of Calgary.

The information although meek, could very well lead the three of them to the Apache Kid and Atalmore's Rangers. Two birds with one stone per'se.

"You know, if we manage to fence in the Kid and Atalmore together, we'll be heading back to the Fort with four sons-of-bitches to feed and watch over," Riley pointed out as they traversed.

"That is what we'll have all right."

"You fellas don't honestly think either of those men ain't going to give up their lives, before we'll ever bring them all in alive, do yous?" Colby wanted to know.

"I'd like to bring them in alive, but, you are right, the chances of that happening without bloodshed are slim. We'll do what we can though, that is all we can do isn't it?" Tyrell responded.

He knew of course it wasn't going to be easy nor was it going to be without spilled blood, he could only hope the blood spilled, wasn't theirs.

"If they was last spotted south-west of Calgary, they'd be heading toward Big Muddy, I can tell you that without doubt."

"Hopefully, we'll get to them before they make the distance. Big Muddy is a week's ride from here, and I don't assume Atalmore or the others have horses with wings. They won't make the distance in a couple weeks from where they're at. Which will give us a couple of weeks to find them," Tyrell inhaled deeply and nodded, "we don't find them before then, we'll head south ourselves. And I can assure you Big Muddy won't be a walk in a daisy field in the middle of winter."

Colby chuckled.

"You got that right, Travis. Yes sir."

"Our best bet at this time of year is to head north up to Chase, and from there straight east to that little train town called Golden Hills, I think," Riley said as they continued northerly. "From there Calgary is pretty close, could make that distance from Golden Hills to Calgary in three or four days I reckon."

"Or less if we hop a train," Tyrell suggested.

"Nope, I won't do that, Travis. I don't want to ride the rails ever again. Coming to Willow Gate by train has given me enough nightmares to last a life time."

"That is 'cause you came through the Rockies. From Golden Hills to Calgary there ain't no mountains as big as the Rockies," Tyrell pointed out.

"It makes no never-mind; I don't want to ride a train, Travis."

"Our only other solution then Riley, is to ride hard and steady for at least a week. We'd be damn close to Calgary by then."

"We'd get there three or four days quicker by train," Colby said as they continued.

"I'd rather ride the distance then hop any damn train. You two want to take one, feel free. I certainly ain't going to join yous. I'll stick to horse and saddle, thank you very much."

Colby and Tyrell both chuckled.

"There ain't any point in arguing with ya, Riley. We'll do it your way," Tyrell said. He was already scheming up a plan, and all it would take was to get Riley drunk. "Once we get to Golden Hills we'll spend a night and gather gear, maybe get another wire off to Ed, to let him know where we are and where we're heading."

"I won't argue that. We'll certainly need some gear to go traipsing through the mountains. I know we is running low on substance, coffee, and such."

The three men continued onward.
In the town of Wheat Field close to the British Columbia border, Barclay Atalmore and his Rebel Ranger's, Spence Hamilton, and Allan Webber were pulling up to the horse pole outside the Wheat Field Hotel. They had been running hard and steady for the past couple of days, and were now counting on some whisky, food, and a good night sleep.

"All right men, we'll rest the night here and pick up in the morning. We ain't that far from the British Columbia border, we should be in the British Columbians by late evening tomorrow night or the next."

Barclay and his men swung off their horses and tethered them.

"All I want is a hot cooked meal and whisky. This little excursion has worn me out," Allan Webber, Barclay Atalmore's second in command spoke out.

"I'll second that," said Spence Hamilton.

"And that is exactly what we're going to get," Barclay Atalmore commented as the three of them entered the hotel. Making their way to the front desk they booked three rooms and baths and then headed to the saloon.

Finding a single table, they sat down with heavy sighs, ordered whisky and some hot food. It didn't take long for their meals to come, and once finished with those, they ordered more whisky to wash it all down.

"I'm quite surprised we made it this far without one damn confrontation from the law. It is a damn good thing we've stuck to the mountains. I reckon if we'd have gone any other way, we'd have had a shoot out by now."

Barclay slugged back his shot of whisky.

"We ain't in the clear yet, Atalmore. We have a few weeks ride ahead, anything can happen."

"True as that might be Web, I have a sneaking hunch we'll make Big Muddy, and once there we'll be in the clear. I ain't worried. We stick to the mountain trails along the U.S. border and we'll be fine."

Spence chuckled.

"That is all conjecture, Atalmore. We can't say a damn thing about being in the clear until we are in the clear."

"You're so damn negative, Spence, you know that?"

"It ain't negativity at all. It is common sense is what that is."

"Well, you're common sense seems to me to be negativity. We've almost made half the distance to Big Muddy and we've not seen one damn redcoat."

"And that means what?" Spence questioned Webber. "It certainly don't mean that the redcoats ain't looking for us."

"You can bet that they is, Spence. But they ain't looking in the right places are they?"

"Again, conjecture. We don't know if we've been followed or not. Or if there ain't a damn redcoat whose going to soon be pulling on our coat tails," Spence chuckled at his own pun.

"The two of you need to quit bickering like old ladies. What we know is this, we've come all this way, and we're getting closer to the U.S. border and destination Big Muddy everyday and we ain't been approached by any redcoat, nor have we seen one. In addition, as far as we can tell we ain't been followed by any either. That there is luck, the deeper we get into the interiors the luckier we'll get.

That is our goal, to get down south as inconspicuously as possible, and then head east right along the Canadian and U.S.A., border which is why we've been traveling as we have been, Spence, to avoid any possible confrontation from the law."

"You don't think the redcoats ain't going to figure that out, Atalmore? The law ain't stupid, what we're doing is what any damn escaped prisoner would do, and that is avoid what it is we've been avoiding. C'mon, you, me and Web, were once lawmen ourselves, how many times did you track down a bad guy? And how long was it before you started looking for him in all the right places?"

There was no arguing what Spence pointed out.

"You made a damn fine point there, Spence, yes indeed. However, it don't change the fact that the redcoats up here in Canada are far a few between. We ain't in the U.S.A. Where every little bow hick cattle town, from east to west, ain't got a lawman of some sort. That is our advantage."

Web chuckled as he looked at Spencer.

"Now, is what he says," Webber started as he gestured to Atalmore with his chin. "Conjecture, Spence?"

Spence was about to respond when an old lady walking with a cane approached them, and she knocked on the underside of the table with it. The men looked at her somewhat confused.

"Yous three the ones that rode in not long ago, and booked rooms and baths?" the old lady asked as she spit a wad of chewing tobacco in the spittoon she held in her left hand. "If you is the baths is ready, three tubs full." Without saying another word, she turned and carried on back the way she came.

"Goddamn, I guess that ends this party. Let's get cleaned up." Barclay Atalmore stood up and headed for his bath, followed close behind by Spence and Webber.

As the three men soaked and scrubbed, conversation turned to the Tallman brothers, Stan and Steve.

"You think those two brothers you hired to find that Travis fellow, have made any headway?" Spence questioned as he slid under the water to rinse his head off. Running his hands now through his hair, he looked over to Atalmore, waiting for an answer.

"Ah, yes, the Tellman brothers, Stan and Steve," Atalmore chuckled. "I doubt they could find a whore house. If they have made any headway, they probably had to change their undershorts a few times. My hope is they are dead. I set them two up, never did like either one," Atalmore commented as he looked into the mirror he held, and continued to run his straight razor across his whiskered face.

"Dead?" Spence looked on somewhat confused. "Why the hell would you want them dead?"

"It is a long story Spence, someday I'll tell you about it. I will tell you why I sent them."

Atalmore splashed water onto his face and looked at Spence.

"I sent them to find Travis all right, but, I knew they could never take him in and most likely their mouths would get them shot, by whom I sent them to look for. My thought had always been to keep my eyes opened for news about them being killed. Once I heard that, and knew where, I'd know where we'd be able to find that son-of-a-bitch known as Travis Sweet," Atalmore smiled. "Or in the least know where to start looking."

"That is diabolical, Atalmore, but damn funny I'll give you that," Webber spoke out with a chuckle.

Spence though, only shook his head.

"So you get two men killed to find one? I agree with Webber, that is diabolical, but it ain't funny."

"What the hell do you mean? Of course it is funny, Spence. I'd say well thought out too. Think about it. I sent two incompetent men to track down that bounty hunter whom sent us three to the clink, and God knows whatever became of Colby. We hear somewhere along the way about the killings of the Tellman's by a single gunman, odds would be good that they were killed by Travis."

"Uh-huh, so that is your genius at work? Again, conjecture. How the hell would you know they were killed by that Travis fellow or not?"

"Can't ever be sure of that," Atalmore began as he stood up from his tub and dried himself off.

"I do know them boys well enough to know they'll not stop looking for Travis until they're dead or they miraculously do manage to bring him to Big Muddy. You see, Spence either way, they'll be killed or they'll do a lot of groundwork for us in finding Travis. It is a win-win."

"For an ex Ranger, Atalmore you sure are a prick." Spence said as he dried himself and dressed.

Webber was sitting on the bench already dressed he had nothing to add to the conversation, nor did he care. Whatever it was that Atalmore planned was fine by him, Atalmore was no fool and nine out of ten times his plans always came to fruition. He didn't work his way up the ranks of the U.S.A. Rangers because he was stupid, Barclay Atalmore was a different kind of man than that.

One hundred and fifty miles west of Wheat Field where Barclay Atalmore and his two men were held up, was Tyrell and the others. They were setting up for the evening. It had been a long day and they were weary from the ride. The flames from their fire danced back and forth, as they conversed. Black Dog lay near, alerted by one sound or another he perked up his ears, sat up and stared into the darkness that lie past the glowing flames.

"What has got into you Black Dog?" Tyrell asked as he noted the dog alerted and on guard. He looked in the same direction, as did the others. They saw nothing except blackness. Finally, Black Dog lay back down. It was a sure sign that there was no threat.

"Ah, must've picked up the scent of a deer or something, eh?" Tyrell pat him. "Good boy, Black Dog, alert and guard," he said as he poured himself a coffee. Gesturing to the others if they too wanted a refill, he poured them each a cup.

"Thanks, Travis," Colby said as he took his cup and looked into the flames, his mind adrift with his own personal battles.

Riley noting this took a swig from his cup and looked over to Colby.

"What's got you all hum-drum, Colby?"

"It ain't nothing, just thinking is all."

"Uh-huh, about what?"

"My cousins back at Cross's place. I never thought I'd miss them."

"Shit it has only been a week or so, since we left them."

"I know that Riley. Still, I wonder what they've been up to."

"Probably the same as they were when we left," Tyrell suggested.

"Yeah, I reckon you is right. At least we don't have to worry about that bastard Gabe Roy causing them any grief."

Colby took a sip from the tin cup in his hands.

"Nope, sure don't have to worry about that none. Besides, I don't suppose Bash or Cannon have even vacated Willow Gate yet. They have a lot of work to do to make things right and bring law and order to that damn town. I tell ya, I don't envy them any."

Tyrell sucked on an eyetooth as he averted his eyes to the fire.

"In time, once we make it back to the Fort, if Bash and Cannon are there, I'm sure they'll be able to tell us how Alex and the others are getting along. I wouldn't worry about them much they can handle themselves. They'll be fine," Tyrell assured. Pulling a package of cheroots out of his pocket, he offered one to both Riley and Colby, only Riley accepted. Colby didn't want to start the nasty habit.

"None for me Travis, I'd rather not muck up my lungs with cat-gut, if you had a whisky though, I'd certainly oblige."

"Nope, ain't got no whisky. Not until we make Golden Hills, maybe we'll get a couple bottles to stuff in our saddle-bags then," Tyrell said as he took a long pull on the cigar dangling from his mouth.

Riley stood up, "I think I got a half bottle tucked away. Hang on." He dug through his saddlebags and produced a half bottle.

"I'd say it is about half full," he handed it to Colby. Who poured a splash into his coffee and handed the bottle back.

"You'd rather add that whisky to your coffee then take a manly swallow?" Riley teased as he pulled the cork and took a slug.

"I ain't looking at getting drunk Riley, only wanted something to curb the lil' twinge of pain I'm feeling from that bullet wound I got back at Cross's place."

"That's still bothering you some?"

"Every now and again, it ain't nothing to worry about though I don't reckon. I'm pretty much healed of it."

Colby took a swallow of his whisky and coffee, and smacked his lips as he wrinkled up his nose and frowned.

"That right there is some awful tasting whisky you got Riley."

"Hell, it is as good as any whisky," Riley responded as he took another pull from the bottle. Wiping his sleeve across his mouth, he handed the bottle over to Tyrell.

"Yuck, I'd have to agree with Colby there Riley, that is awful gut rot."

Regardless of how awful it was it didn't take long before the bottle was empty. The men now half-drunk began singing silly songs around their fire, laughing and joking as they did. Black Dog sat vigilantly. If he could speak, he'd tell them how stupid they looked. Finally, with a last hoorah and a few more minutes of garbled conversation, the men rolled out their bedrolls. Another night on the trail had ended.

Chapter 4

It was mid-day on December 28 when the three of them came across a little town that wasn't on the map they carried. The town sign simply read 'Nowhere- Population 19' and below that it read '2 miles'.

They slowed their horse down to read the sign.

"Ain't never heard of this place, 'Nowhere', Jesus what kind of name is that for a town?"

"One that is out in the middle of nowhere, I'd assume," Colby said with a smirk.

"Maybe we can get us a warm room for the night and some food. I don't reckon a town with a population of nineteen is going to have much more than a few shanties and maybe a small hotel."

"We ain't going to know for sure until we get there. A couple of miles to go. C'mon, let's get," Riley said as the three men heeled their horses and continued on, Black Dog trailing close behind.

The road into town hadn't been travelled on for a while, it had snowed recently, but with the little amount that came down, anyone who had trod into Nowhere would have left a trail of sorts. However, there was nothing, no track leading into or leaving.

A few minutes later, the small town of Nowhere appeared in the distance. From where they were, they could faintly make out a couple of buildings that were dilapidated and in disarray.

"I'd say Nowhere is a ghost town," Tyrell spoke as they approached.

"From the look of it, I wouldn't argue," Riley responded as they drew close.

Finally making the distance, the three men looked around. The hotel was the only building that remained standing with a roof. Some of the windows had broken out over the years and only a few panes of glass had remained. The other buildings had all caved in. They were in such disarray that the only thing they'd be good for was firewood. Nowhere, was certainly a ghost town.

Swinging off their saddles, they tethered their horses to the old horse pole outside the hotel.

"Let's take a look around," Tyrell said as he scouted the area.

Behind the hotel was a small graveyard and chapel that had been taken care of over the years. Still they too were on their last legs of appeal. The rest of the town itself was a wreck.

"Sure makes a man wonder what might have happened here," Colby pointed out as they continued looking around.

"It is a wonder, indeed. It is interesting to see that chapel and graveyard have been looked after, everything else, well, it is all gone," Riley said as they made their way to the front of the hotel.

Creaking open the door they step inside. There were tables and chairs against the far wall and an old wood burning stove sat alone against another, there was some firewood stacked next to that.

The saloon floor was covered in a layer of dust and a few mice scattered as they walked in further. The old six-stool bar still had the stools lined up, and they made their way over and sat down as they looked around.

"I reckon we could hold up here for the night. I hope that that old wood stove can still be fired up. I think tonight is going to be cold."

Tyrell stood up and opened another door that led to a set of stairs.

"Looks like there might be a few rooms upstairs, let's go have a look."

Colby and Riley followed.

The hotel had only five rooms and each one was completely void of any furnishings, and it caused their voices to echo slightly as they talked. Opening one of the closet doors it fell off its hinges. Riley leaned it up against the wall. Inside were a few knick-knacks and old bed linens that had become a home to some kind or vermin, likely rats.

"Yuk, it stinks like rat piss, don't it?' Colby said as he stepped back.

"I reckon that is what lives here. I wonder what they get charged per night," Riley joked.

Finished with their tour upstairs they headed back down to the saloon.

"I say we gather our gear and make ourselves comfy for the night. I reckon there is enough wood to get the fire started, could probably cook on it too, or at least get some coffee going."

Tyrell walked over to the wood stove and gave it the once over.

"Yeah, I think we can fire this old stove up. The chimney looks fine, she's still pretty solid."

Satisfied, they gathered their gear and settled in. They pulled a table and three chairs out and set them up near the wood stove. Tyrell added water from his canteen to the coffee pot and adding grinds he set it down to perk.

"This will be a fine place to spend the night. Keeps us out of the weather at least," Tyrell pulled up a chair.

"I don't think the wood we have is going to keep us going all night, we'll have to gather some more, I think," he added.

"That'll be easy enough we could rip some away from one of the old buildings. Saves us the trouble of foraging for it, unless of course some is stacked out back, I never noticed any, but then again I wasn't looking either," standing Colby exited. A few minutes later, he came back with an arm full of wood.

"As suspected, there is a stack out back."

He tossed the wood on the pile.

"There that ought to get us through. How is that coffee coming Travis?" he asked as he sat back down.

"The stove ain't even putting off any heat yet, Colby. I don't think it'll be much longer though."

Riley who had stretched out his legs and tilted his hat over his face was snoring, and Colby kicked his chair.

"Jesus Christ, Riley, you sound like a damn barn animal with that snoring of yours. Quit it!"

Riley mumbled a few obscenities and went right back to snoring.

Both Tyrell and Colby shook their heads.

"Ah, let him sleep Colby, he's old."

"His damn snoring is making the roof rafters shake. He sounds like a damn Goose."

"That'd be a Gander," Tyrell corrected him.

"Goose, Gander, I don't care which, but he sounds like one or the other," Colby chuckled.

In the distance less than half a mile away, an old rancher had noticed smoke rising from the town of Nowhere.

His first thought was that the Shepherd had returned. When he was around, he often stayed in Nowhere. He didn't know if that was the young Indian's name or not, but, he and a few other ranchers in the area named him that. He was responsible for the deaths of a dozen would be cattle rustlers.

He never stayed long in one spot. He had only been spotted on a few occasions, the ranchers though kept that to themselves. The Shepherd as far as they were concerned was doing them a just service. The dead men who were found over the years were, identified by the law as cattle rustlers. Each shot with a .50 caliber ball, and that was the only lead the law had.

The old rancher's name was Lendale Pitts, and he was about to be reacquainted with an old friend of his. Taking one last long pull from the pipe, he held in his hand, he set it down in the pipe holder. Slipping on his boots and heavy jacket, he made his way over to the bunkhouse, it wasn't too late yet and he didn't want to go alone to Nowhere in case who he thought might be there wasn't and someone else was. Gathering up two of his cattle hands, they armed themselves, saddled their horse and the three men headed to Nowhere.

"You think it might be the Shepherd?" one of his men asked.

"Hard to say Tooley, I don't recall him ever being in the area this late in the year. If it is, he'll let us know by stepping out. Other than that, I'm not sure," Lendale half chuckled. "But, since I am the ambassador, if you will, of Nowhere, I'd like to check up on things."

Lendale and his family when they were young once lived in Nowhere. Then when the epidemic hit killing one of his sons and crippling his wife, who later succumbed to the illness, he moved what was left of his family a half a mile away. Promising those that survived and were leaving behind Nowhere, that he would maintain the chapel and graveyard of which most of their kin were buried for as long as he was able. For the past fifteen years that is exactly, what he did as the town itself slowly crumbled to the ground and the grasslands and forest encroached.

"What are we going to do if it ain't him?" the second man asked.

"If there is no harm being done, then no foul I guess." Lendale replied.

It was a well-known fact that Nowhere had often served as a place of refuge for travelers and as long as things weren't being wrecked or ruin, most folks in the area didn't seem to care. Nor did Lendale Pitts; however, there were times when he and a handful of his men chased the uncouth off. He hoped this wasn't one of those times. They were only three.

Most of Pitts' men were home with their wives and children during the winter holidays. Although all lived on the Pitts' land, he felt no need to rouse them. If things looked suspicious the closer they got, he'd send Tooley or Underhill to gather more men.

"I don't hear no hooting or hollering, like what one might hear, I don't think Nowhere has been taken over by whisky drunkards. Likely passers-by, needing a place for the night, we'll know soon enough," Lendale said as the three of them continued.

Finally, Nowhere came into view and from where they rode into town they could see three horses tethered.

"Three riders it looks like," Tooley said as they approached closer.

"Well, at least our odds are good."

"We can't know that Underhill until we lock eyes with those inside the hotel."

It was then Black Dog began barking at the oncoming riders. Holding his ground, he stood by the hotel door.

Tyrell and Colby both stood up, leaving Riley to sleep, he didn't move a muscle, and if he wasn't snoring, one might think he was dead.

"Sounds like something is awry," Tyrell said as he and Colby headed toward the door and exited onto the old boardwalk. In the distance, they saw three riders approaching. Tyrell got Black Dog to quiet down and he looked over to Colby who was standing beside him.

"Best go wake up Riley, I ain't sure what is coming."

"With pleasure," Colby said as he went inside. He grabbed the back of the chair that Riley was sitting on, shook it like a madman, until Riley slid off, and landed with a thud on the floor.

"We got riders coming," he said with a chuckle.

"Jesus Christ, Colby, you could've broken my back," Riley wasn't impressed. Colby reached down and helped him up off the floor.

"No time to belly ache about your damn back. I would have thought you'd have fluttered your wings, Geese can fly can't they?"

"Geese? What the hell are you talking about?" Riley asked as he dusted himself off.

"That is what you sound like when you're snoring," Colby responded as he and Riley headed out.

The three approaching riders by now were close and they pulled their horses up next to the boardwalk.

"Evening. My name is…" Lendale began as Riley recognized him.

"Lendale," Riley looked closer, "Lendale Pitts! My sweet Jesus is that you?"

By now, Lendale had also recognized Riley and he swung off his horse.

"Riley Scott, you old son-of-a-bitch," Lendale said as he met Riley and the two shook hands.

"How many years has it been?"

"Damn near twenty I think. You don't look any different than you did back then. How the hell have you been Lendale?"

"As good as twenty years can be on any man, who you got with you Riley?" Lendale asked as he looked at both Tyrell and Colby.

"Shit, sorry about that Lendale, this is Travis and Colby."

Both Tyrell and Colby nodded their acknowledgement.

Lendale shook both their hands.

"Nice to meet yous."

"Nice to meet you too, Lendale, was it?" Tyrell asked as he shook his hand.

"Yes, sir. Lendale Pitts."

"Mr. Pitts and you men on them horses, nice to meet you, but, Travis, Riley I ain't too interested in standing in the cold reminiscing. So, I'm going back inside where the wind don't blow," Colby said as he turned heel and went back inside.

"You might as well join us Lendale, Colby is right it is a lot cozier inside," Riley said as he gestured to Lendale and his men.

"We got coffee on."

Lendale looked back to Tooley and Underhill.

"You men feel like a cup of coffee?"

"Ah, if it is all right by you Lendale, me and Tooley will head back. We ain't needed here."

Lendale nodded.

"All right, I'll see yous in the morning, I'm going to stick around and have a coffee."

The two men turned their horses and headed back the way they came, leaving Lendale to reacquaint himself with his old friend Riley.

Making their way inside the old run down and dilapidated hotel, the four of them sat down.

Riley poured Lendale a coffee and handed it to him.

"So, Lendale, what are you doing in these parts? I thought you lived down southerly."

"We did for a while then I moved the wife and kids here, to Nowhere. I bought a rock quarry and started supplying the Rail Road with shale to lay down with the tracks."

"How are your wife and kids? Those two young whippersnappers must be all grown up by now."

Lendale took a swallow from his coffee and looked around. There was a time when Nowhere was on the threshold of being a start up town. Then the red plague came and wiped out most of the folks and their kin. The surviving town folk packed up and left. Lendale's wife and one of his sons both succumbed to the plague, and died. They were both buried in the small graveyard behind the hotel, and that was the reason Lendale had been taking care of it for as long as he had.

He looked now back to Riley and smiled bleakly.

"The wife and Edgar my youngest died right here in Nowhere. The red plague came through here and wiped out most of the folks and their kin, some fifteen years ago or longer, it was shortly after I bought the rock quarry."

Lendale took another swig from his coffee as he reminisced.

"Sorry to hear that Lendale, my condolences," Riley responded with sincerity.

"Thank you Riley, but, it was a long time ago and an ugly time for those of us that lived around here. I've been the caretaker of the chapel and graveyard ever since. When I saw smoke rising from the hotel smoke stack, I figured it be best that I take a gander. Make sure things weren't being burned up."

"So this town has been a ghost town for fifteen years or better?" Colby now questioned.

"That is right, for fifteen long years not a soul has lived here. On occasion though this place has been used by travelers like yourself to seek shelter and refuge from the weather and such. There are myself, and a couple of ranchers that live nearby. Other than that, the town folk that survived the plague and lived here moved on. Nowhere was going to be a railroad town, there was big hope for it. But, when the tracks turned west instead of continuing south that hope died, shortly after that is when the plague came."

"Never heard of the red plague before," Colby responded.

"I ain't sure that is the medical term for it, but that is what we called it. It turned the skin of the ailing a red color, almost like a sunburn if you will. That was the first symptom, then their skin would bleed little droplets of blood and eventually they died. The process took a few days, but we all knew the outcome.

It was hard to watch our kin and loved ones suffering through it. It seemed to hit the women folk first, and from there it spread. Some of us were lucky of course and managed not to get sick. But, after it was all over there weren't many of us left, myself and oldest along with a six others are all that survived."

Lendale lowered his head and nodded.

"It was a bad time."

"Well then, let's not talk about it anymore, Lendale," Riley responded knowing how difficult it seemed to be for Lendale to bring up.

Lendale waved his hand through the air.

"Ah, I can talk about it now. There was a time though I would have rather not. For now, let's talk about you Riley. You still bringing in bounties?"

"I am. I work for McCoy's out of the Fort. So, do Travis here and Colby."

"All three of you are bounty hunters then?"

"For now least wise."

"Yeah, I've read that Canada is no longer going to offer support to your craft come next year, is there any truth to that Riley?" Lendale questioned.

"There is truth to that, indeed Lendale. It ain't so much that bounty hunting is going to be expelled from Canada, more like we're all going to be under new ruling. Bounty hunters are no longer bounty hunters in the sense that we used to be. Come next year we're considered Private Investigators and Security personnel. With a list of laws, we have to respect. Not much different actually, than the redcoats list of laws, the only difference being is that we can be hired by civilians and governing agencies to do private investigations, security details and what not."

"Hired lawmen in other words?"

"Not quite, but close," Riley stood up and poured each of them another coffee as they continued conversing.

It was during that time while conversing that Lendale mentioned the Shepherd.

"So an almost Indian fella has been living here at times, and takes down cattle rustlers?" Colby questioned.

"I wouldn't say he wasn't an Indian, I'd say he is. From what I've seen of him, he dresses not much different than the Athabasca in the area. So, I assume he's an Indian."

Lendale took a swig from his coffee.

"He certainly ain't feared by those of us that live around here. He's done good work at knocking down would be cattle rustlers, and has saved us from that hardship of losing cattle. The law don't even know who he is. He comes and goes."

"You say he uses an old lead ball muzzleloader?" Tyrell questioned next.

"That is what the dead have been killed by. A .50 caliber lead ball don't allow for any missing, so he is a damn fine shot too."

"Humph, well that is interesting. I don't know if I ever heard of an Indian shooting cattle rustlers before. Yet, not bring harm to anyone else. Seems odd to me."

"Odd as it may seem, that is what the Shepherd does. It don't make much sense to any of us either, but we don't chase him off when he's about. We let him be, and he leaves us alone. He's never even stolen a chicken."

Tyrell knew that the three of them were thinking the same thing. Was the Shepherd, Lendale spoke of, by chance the Apache Kid? Only problem was what they knew of the Apache Kid, was that he himself had been deemed a cattle rustler. It could be of course that the Shepherd was not who they thought him to be. But, the fact about the .50 caliber muzzleloader that the Shepherd used was known to also be the Apache Kid's preferred weapon; a .50 caliber Hawken. Coincidence?

"When was the last time that the Shepherd was here, in Nowhere?"

Lendale finished his coffee and set the cup down.

"The last time I think was this past fall. I never seen him, but old man Tweedsmuir did. He told me the Shepherd glided across his field like a ghost on a white horse. Some things though, old man Tweedsmuir says has to be taken with a grain of salt. He is a bit on the peculiar side of things himself," Lendale chuckled.

"So, a few months ago, then?" Riley reiterated.

"If what Tweedsmuir says is true, anyway, Riley, my coffee is finished and I should get back to the house before it gets dark. If you folks want, before you leave here in the morning, I can have my housemaid put together a good home cooked breakfast. Come by my place in the morning, you can't miss it. You'll see the sign that says Pitts Rock Quarry."

Lendale stood up from the table and shook Riley's hand again.

"It's been nice seeing you again, Riley, and I hope you'll take my offer of a good home cooked meal before you folks leave here."

Riley smiled and nodded.

"You can count on that Lendale. Ain't one of us been fed a good meal in a while, we ain't about to turn that down."

Riley walked Lendale to the door and stepped out with him.

"What time in the morning should we show up for breakfast?" Riley asked as Lendale swung up onto his horse.

"Any time in the morning is fine, whether breakfast has been served or not, I'll make sure you three don't leave hungry."

Lendale chuckled as he turned his horse and heeled its flanks.

"I'll see you folks in the morning Riley."

"You bet. Thanks Lendale, we'll see you then," Riley, answered back as he watched his old friend heading home. Turning now, he went back inside and sat again at the table.

"What do you two make of this Shepherd, Lendale spoke of?" he asked as he poured another coffee.

"How many Indians in these parts do you figure pack around a .50 caliber?" Colby questioned as much as pointed out.

"I think that is the giveaway right there. Some would be packing around those lunkers, but not many. Could be the Shepherd is that of whom we seek," Tyrell commented.

"Say he is, after listening to Lendale and how highly he and the others in this area look upon him, would you still want to bring him in?"

"We have to, Colby. That is our job," Riley paused as he took a swallow from the coffee in his hands.

"Nope, I don't think so Riley. If we never saw him how could we bring him in?"

"That right there Colby, goes against everything the oath we swore to when we took on this type of work. It is our duty as such, to act accordingly and follow the laws we agreed to uphold. The Apache Kid is a wanted felon and we've been appointed the task to apprehend him. That is our job."

"I know all about that, Riley. The thing is, after hearing your old friend Lendale Pitts, talk about the fella he and the others in these parts call the Shepherd as he did, makes a man wonder if what one hears is always true. Say the Shepherd and the Kid is one of the same, it would seem to me that he's been doing more good than bad. Wouldn't you agree?"

"What a man is today and what a man was yesterday, if that man is a wanted felon doesn't change the fact that he's a wanted man. The only time it changes is when the law courts find him not guilty on the charges he is wanted for or has paid for those crimes."

Riley stirred in his chair and stretched out his legs.

"Trust me though, Colby, I know what you mean. There are many men, who have paid with their lives, in one form or the other, and were never guilty of anything. That is why we have a court of law, judges, jurors, prosecutors, and lawyers. It is always the hope that the not guilty are proven to be just that."

"Of course that is why, only thing is that ain't how it always turns out for the not guilty," Colby responded.

Tyrell, who had been sitting idle listening to the two, hadn't much more to add to the conversation. He understood Colby's point and Riley's too. He himself fit into both categories, he was a wanted felon under the guise of Travis Sweet, and at the same- time, not guilty, of what he had been accused. He finally chimed in.

"We can't be certain one way or the other if the Shepherd and the Kid are the same man. Commonsense tells us that it likely is, and so do my own instincts, but until we can be certain we really can't make any judgment of guilt or innocence.

What we do have, are a few new facts and coincidences that add up to two things. One there is an Indian that has been killing cattle rustlers, has a .50 caliber Hawken, which coincidentally is the same as what we know the Apache Kid uses, two, or maybe three whichever, he rides a white horse.

I think what we should do, is maybe have a talk with that Tweedsmuir fellow. Lendale mentioned he claimed to have seen the Shepherd not long ago."

"He also said Tweedsmuir is a bit off center," Riley pointed out as he continued looking at his outstretched legs and boots with his hat tilted over his eyes.

"Most times I think you is off center too, Riley," Colby chuckled. "I think you is right Travis, we should have a chat with Tweedsmuir."

"I wasn't disagreeing. I was only pointing out the other aspect about talking to a man who is otherwise peculiar. We can't go talk to him now," Riley yawned and inhaled deeply, he was tired. "We'll ask Lendale on whereabouts we can find him at breakfast."

"I reckon so," Tyrell stood up and added a few more pieces of wood to the stove. No sooner had he sat back down and Riley was already snoring.

"Jesus Christ, are we going to have to listen to that rumble all night," Colby shook his head.

"Give his chair a kick, he'll shut up," Tyrell smiled.

"Nah, the last time I woke him he seemed a little bit pissed off. Next time he might shoot." Both Colby and Tyrell chuckled.

A short while later the empty saloon echoed with the snores of three men.

Chapter 5

The next morning, Riley was the first to rise. It was still dark out and he added wood to the stove, the embers still glowed and it didn't take long for the place to warm up. He looked over to where both Tyrell and Colby were sprawled out wrapped up in their bedrolls. Their snoring, the only sound other than the gentle crackling of the fire and the wind outside. It was maddening and he walked over to where they lay and jumped up and down. The floorboards echoed their age as both men woke up to the rumbling sound.

"Goddamn it, Riley! What the hell?" Tyrell exclaimed as he sat up and rubbed his eyes. Colby on the other hand simply looked up unimpressively and shook his head.

"The two of you snoring was ruining my peace and quiet that I'm accustomed too in the wee hours of morning. Since I'm first up, and have the fire going nicely, one of you can gather me some snow so I can get coffee going. Need a cup before we head to Lendale's place."

Colby reached over to his stack of gear and slid a canteen across the floor to where Riley stood.

"Filled that up yesterday, should be enough in there to make coffee."

"Well, thank you very much Colby," Riley responded as he picked it up and proceeded to make coffee.

In the little amount of time it took to roll up their bedding and gather their gear, the coffee was done. Sitting down they each poured themselves a cup.

"There is nothing like a hot coffee in the morning to put the poop back into a weary man," Riley said as he took a swig.

"Or on the other hand, make a man poop," Colby chuckled, as did both Riley and Tyrell.

"Full of wit this morning eh, Colby?"

"Ah, he's full of something, might not be wit though."

This remark made by Riley only made the three of them chuckle louder. It was going to be one of those days.

Black Dog, who by now heard the men and their raucous chuckles, came traipsing down the stairs. Unaware that he had ever been inside with them, the three men were startled. Colby whose back was to the sound, spun around the pistol given to him by Crying Wolf was grasped in his hand. Not Riley or even Tyrell had seen him draw it.

"Jesus Christ, Colby you drew that fast. No worries though it is only Black Dog," Tyrell said as the dog came over to him and sat.

"Morning Black Dog, I had no idea you was in here with us last night. Must've found a cozy corner to lie down in eh? You snuck in when the door was opened, didn't ya?" Tyrell scratched the dog behind the ear.

"Now back to how quickly you drew that colt, Colby, where the hell did you learn that?"

"To tell you the truth, Travis, I ain't got a clue. It seemed natural," Colby too was shocked at the speed in which he pulled the pistol.

"Natural? Shit, it takes a man a long time and a lot of practice to pull a pistol that quick," Riley commented.

Colby shrugged.

"Don't know what to tell either of yous. That was the first time I pulled a pistol."

"Well, you did it damn fast. See if you can do it again, Colby," Tyrell encouraged.

"All right," Colby stood up.

"You want me to draw it now, or do you want to count to three?" Colby wanted to know, he was as interested in seeing if he could do it again, or not, as much as the others.

Without rhyme or reason, Riley hollered at the top of his lungs, "now!" and just as quickly Colby, had the pistol grasped in his right hand.

He looked at the others his eyes big with surprise. "Goddamn, that was easy, maybe some kind of Athabasca magic or something, I don't know."

Tyrell and Riley simply leaned back in their chairs and looked on. They were both dumbfounded at how quickly Colby was able to draw the colt.

"That is quite the thing. Jesus, if you've never drawn a pistol before, then it is either magic or as you say natural. Think you could hit anything though?"

"Can't say either way, Travis, we should test that," Colby said with sincerity. "The only way we'll know is to go out and lean up an old board or something that I can shoot at. Maybe my draw is good but my aim is bad."

Riley and Tyrell chuckled.

"Could be you are right. Let's go see what you can do," Riley stood from the table followed by Tyrell, and the three men along with Black Dog exited into the rising sun. Finding an old board Tyrell stuck it in the snow. He walked back to where Colby and Riley were standing, a few yards away.

"There you go Colby, see if you can put lead in that board."

"How far away do you figure it is Travis? Looks like I could spit on it from here."

"Let's move back some then, sixty feet, or so."

"Sixty feet? That is a might close ain't it?" Colby questioned.

"Not so much for a colt. Nope. It is a good distance, anytime you're going to need to use a pistol is going to be close. Go on, draw that .45, and shoot the board," Tyrell pushed, if Colby could hit the board as quickly as he could draw, he and Riley would certainly be impressed.

Colby turned a bit this way, and a bit that way, until finally he found his pose. Then as though a bullwhip had been cracked, he pulled out the colt aimed and fired. That was his mistake. Not Riley or Tyrell wanted to point that out to him yet. They wanted to see if he could learn that on his own, the best teacher was always experience.

"Damn, the barrel must be crooked. I aimed right at that board," Colby was a bit disappointed. "I'm going to try again."

Two, three, four shots later and the board didn't move, not a splinter of wood punched into the snow.

"There you have it. I can't aim worth shit with this thing, can draw it quick, but can't hit a damn thing."

"How about this time, you don't aim at all, simply point and shoot," Riley suggested.

Colby frowned a bit and then smiled. He understood now. Nodding, he took up his pose again and loosening his shoulders, he drew the .45 and fired. Splinters of wood now scattered the snow and the board fell over. A smile crossed his face as he turned and looked over to where Tyrell and Riley stood.

"So that is the secret? Draw, point, and shoot," Colby spoke not so much as a question but a statement.

"It is. When you're being shot at or facing a man with a pistol in his hand, things are different. Here is a tip for you- never fear another man with a pistol if you are armed as well, 'cause chances are he's the one who is afraid," Tyrell informed.

"Or as afraid," Riley added.

Colby by now was reloading his .45.

"I think the two of you forgot another few words of wisdom?"

"Oh, what might those be?" Riley asked.

Colby looked over to him as he put the last bullet into the cylinder and he smiled.

"Always reload," he said as he slipped the pistol back into its holster that Tyrell had a spare of and had given to him a few days back.

Tyrell laughed and nodded.

"You got that right. Never put an unloaded gun back in a gun belt."

Riley too chuckled. Colby was right that was as important as being able to draw and shoot.

A few hours later after having breakfast with Lendale and a couple of his hired hands, the three men thanked him for the meal and said their goodbyes, and were now headed east to where the Tweedsmuir ranch was located. They got the directions from Lendale and were now pulling up to the ranch house. It wasn't big, nor was it small. A dozen or so cows ambled in the pen next to the barn.

Dismounting, Tyrell tied his horse to the horse pole. Riley and Colby remained mounted. Walking up to the door and using the doorknocker, he knocked and then stepped back.

"Who is it?" A grumpy voice from the other side answered.

"We're looking for a Joe Tweedsmuir? We're with McCoy's Private Investigations out of the Fort," Tyrell replied.

Finally, the door opened and an aging man dressed in an expensive woolen suit looked at him.

"So, what are you doing on my stoop? What do you want from me?"

"We don't mean to be a bother, mister, we're only looking for some information. We were told by Lendale Pitts, that you saw a fellow riding through here on a white horse this past fall."

"Uh-huh and why would men of your statures want to know something like that? Besides anything Pitts tells ya is probably horse hooey anyway."

"So, you didn't see a man riding through here on a white horse this past fall?" Tyrell questioned.

"I never said that. I asked why you wanted to know. Show me some credentials, for all I know you're cattle rustlers. C'mon show me something that says you isn't."

Tyrell reached into his inside pocked and handed the man his badge and credentials. The man looked closely then handed it back.

"All right so you is law types. Yeah, I saw a man on a white horse this past fall, was the Shepherd. What would you want with him?"

"The man you folks call the Shepherd may be a man we are looking for."

"I already gathered that. Can't see any reason law types might want to find the Shepherd. Give me a reason, or get back onto that horse of yours and get off my land."

"If he is the man we think he is he's also known as the Apache Kid," Riley spoke from his horse.

Joe stepped forward forcing Tyrell to step aside, he stood on his porch and looked at Riley.

"The Apache Kid, you say?"

"That is right," Riley confirmed.

Joe started to laugh.

"The Apache Kid from what I've read in newsprint and have heard is a barbarous maniac. There is no way the Shepherd is he. He ain't an Apache, and certainly not the Apache Kid."

"And you know this how?" Colby spoke up.

"As I told your partner there who is sitting on a horse beside you, the Shepherd isn't Apache, nor is he an Athabasca," Joe blurted.

"I know what you told my partner, and I asked how do you know he ain't? Have you spoken with him, have you broke bread with him? If you haven't than you don't really know do you?"

Joe lowered his head as he contemplated.

"I guess you is right in that respect, I have not spoken with him, nor have I broke bread with him, so as you say young man, you are right I don't know for certain if he is or ain't. What I do know is the Shepherd is harmless, or leastwise hasn't caused anyone in these parts any despair."

"All right so now that we are clear on that, Joe, how about you tell us in what direction the man on the white horse travelled, and we'll let you get back to your doings," Tyrell said as he stepped off the stoop and looked at him.

"He traveled north easterly, toward the Rocky Mountains and the prairies beyond."

Tyrell nodded as he looked in that direction.

"Thank you Joe. We'll let you be now."

Tyrell made his way over to his horse and swung up on the saddle. He looked one more time at Joe and tilting his hat in thanks, the three of them headed north easterly. Joe watched as they vanished from his sight, then stepping back inside he closed the door behind him.

"Shit, that fella seemed to be a bit of an ass, didn't he?" Colby questioned as the three of them continued onward.

"Loneliness and solitude sometimes makes a man miserable, I think that is Joe's problem, he's miserable and lonely. On the other hand, maybe he is an ass, like you say Colby. We can't be sure the Shepherd traveled this way, though, Joe could've been lying through his teeth about that."

"Nah, I don't think he was lying, makes sense that the Shepherd would head this way. If he is the Apache Kid, like we suspect, he's heading directly toward where Atalmore and his Rebel Rangers have been seen, and that was southwest of Calgary. Could be the Rangers and the Shepherd are going to meet up between here and there," Riley pointed out.

"That was a few months ago that the Shepherd supposedly headed this way. He could be anywhere, may have turned directly north. We ain't going to know either way until we find a sign, and at this time of year, any sign is going to be damn hard to come by. The only good thing is Golden Hills is our next stop and it lies in this direction."

It was January 1 1892 when the three riders finally made the distance to Golden Hills; they hadn't found one iota of any evidence regarding the Shepherd as they traveled to the town. That didn't mean however that the Shepherd hadn't traveled that way, it simply meant they hadn't found any sign one-way or the other.

"Here we are fellas, Golden Hills. Not much more of a town than Nowhere," Tyrell said as they dismounted outside the hotel and tethered their horses.

"We going to stay here for the night?" Colby asked as the three of them looked around.

"Not much point in going any further, today. I see down yonder a telegraph office," Riley said as he gestured toward the small building.

"I'll go ahead and send off a wire to the Fort. Maybe by now Ed has some news for us regarding the Apache Kid. You two go ahead and grab us a couple of rooms. I'll meet ya's back here, shortly."

Riley petered off down the boardwalk and entered the small telegraph office. Sending a wire off to Ed, he paid the fee and requested notification if anything came back from the Fort with his name on it. The clerk agreed, if anything from the Fort showed up he'd send someone to inform him. Nodding and thanking the clerk he headed back to the Golden Hills Hotel, and met up with Tyrell and Colby in the saloon.

"Well, that is done," Riley said as he pulled up a chair and sat down. "If anything comes back from the Fort we'll be informed. Did we get rooms?" he asked.

"Not rooms, one room. We're going to have to bunk together. There was only one room available out of the six the hotel has," Colby replied.

"Oh, well least we ain't going to have to spend another cold night out."

"I don't know, I think I'd rather spend the night out than bunk with you, Riley. You snore like a Goddamn son-of-a-bitch, and it is getting tiring."

"Quit your crying about my snoring, Colby, you snore like a Goddamn son-of-a-bitch too."

"Yeah, but at least it don't wake me," Colby chuckled.

Riley smirked and shook his head.

"Do we got whisky coming or what?" he asked.

"That is the other thing, we were informed there ain't no whisky here, was all drunk up last night, during the new year celebrations."

"Jesus Christ, that is right we're into 1892 now, aren't we?"

"Yep, January 1, 1892. Welcome to the new year fellows," Tyrell smiled, "I can't believe how quick this past year went."

"So, we've been on the damn trail for more than ten days and ain't any closer to the purpose of this excursion. I would have thought by now we would have something to show for our efforts. Instead, we are in a one-horse town that is dry of whisky. Not a very good start to a new year," Riley shook his head.

"Ah, don't sweat it Riley, we can drink draft."

"Well then, let's order some. I could use a drink."

Back at the Fort, Ed McCoy was sending a reply back to Riley in Golden Hills. He had no news regarding the Apache Kid- but did have confirmation the Barclay Atalmore and his Rebel Rangers were heading west into the British Columbia interior. He suggested they head west to the town of Wheat Field, the last known location of Atalmore and his men.

With the task done, Ed returned to the McCoy's office and poured himself a coffee. Brady who had celebrated the night before was sick and hung over and wasn't expected to show up at the office that day. With coffee in hand, Ed made his way into his private office and sat down with a heavy sigh. It was hard for him to sit idle and he made himself busy by going through the business financials and prepared them for when Brady took over the business, at the end of January.

He still hadn't told his wife yet on his pending retirement, nor had he mentioned it to Riley or the others who were working abroad out in the field. Only Brady knew and he hadn't said anything either.

With the financials now worked out, Ed leaned back in his chair and looked around his office. It was hard for him to think that soon he'd no longer have a need for it. He had spent a lot of time in that office. It held many memories both good and bad. He smiled solemnly to himself as he reminisced.

In the end, he knew it would all be good. Brady knew the job and the men they had working for them, Tanner McBride, Matt Crawford, Travis Sweet and his old friend Riley Scott, not to mention the youngest member of their crew Colby Christian, he knew were all good men. They could keep the business afloat, Ed was certain of that. Yet it was still hard for him to accept the fact, that one day not to long from then, it would be Brady sitting in his chair.

By now, the clerk from the telegraph office up in Golden Hills had passed the reply from the Fort over to Riley. Who read it and passed it to Tyrell.

"So, nothing new on the Kid, just information on the whereabouts of Atalmore and his men's last location," Tyrell said as he read it.

"Yes sir, Wheat Field," Riley responded with little enthusiasm. "That is another few days ride from here. Damn. I was hoping for something more substantial."

"If you ask me that is pretty substantial, if Atalmore and the others are heading into the interior, why don't we head that way ourselves? I'm sure I know the route they'll be taking to Big Muddy now. They'll be heading along the Columbia River, to Idaho," Colby confirmed.

"How can you be sure of that?" Tyrell asked.

"I've been along that route with them before. If we cut southwest from here, we could make the Columbia River in about three days ride, give, or take. That'd put us on the shores of the Columbia, from there we head south. I know Atalmore and that crew well enough to know, that they're going to be taking all the mountain passes. Likely hop a river boat into the Casino Mountain's, from there it is only a hop, skip, and jump into the U.S.A. That is where we need to go. Could be also we might run across the Kid," Colby was sincere he knew what he was talking about.

Riley took a swig from his third draft beer.

"What makes you think the Kid could be going that way too?"

"Like I told you before, Riley, the Kid and the Rebel Rangers have been in cahoots with each other on occasion, and I know the Kid also travels that route."

"Only thing is Colby, that is the wrong direction that the Kid supposedly traveled, according to Tweedsmuir, and it is west, not easterly as he should be going."

"That don't mean nothing, Travis, who is to say he didn't eventually turn back. He ain't stupid, knows how to avoid detection and leave false trails, as we've already seen."

"I guess you do make a fair point. All right, in the morning we'll head west again. If nothing else, and with some luck, we might in the least be able to bring Atalmore and crew in again."

It was settled.

Chapter 6

Saturday January 2, 1892. The three of them left Golden Hills in the early twilight of dawn and coursed their way south westerly for a distance then turned west on an old wagon trail they found on the map. The snow-covered trail revealed that at least three maybe four riders in all had used the trail before the last snowfall, a few days earlier.

"Looks like since the last snow fall riders have gone through here, four it looks like," Riley pointed out as they carried on.

"Four, eh, ain't that something. Could be them riders is the ones we've been looking for, could be not too," Colby responded as he shrugged.

"The number of riders is right, that is for sure. What are the odds that they're the ones we're looking for? I can't see it being that easy or us being that lucky."

"I was only speculating, Travis."

"I know, but you could be right."

"I suppose, but, like you say how lucky could that be?"

"Never discount luck, 'cause you never know when it is going to show itself," Riley commented as they continued.

At mid-day, they slowed their horses to a halt and decided to rest. They had rode for six hours and were in desperate need of break, and so they took the opportunity now.

"How long you figure we've been on them damn horses?" Riley questioned as he took a swig from his canteen.

"Since sun-up," Colby replied, "and it sure feels good to get off."

"Yeah, and if I was a younger man, I might want to carry on a while longer. I ain't though and it is mid-day now, going to be getting dark soon. I say we settle here for the night," Riley pleaded.

"That is your old bones and age talking, I reckon. I wouldn't argue though. What about you Travis, think we should settle for the evening? Have to admit it is a pretty good spot here."

"I ain't got no quip about that. Here is fine. Let's do it and get settled," Tyrell agreed.

It took a few minutes to settle and with a fire going and coffee on the flames, Riley wanted to know what day it was.

"Either of you know what day it is?" he asked as he stirred the coals.

"Think about that, yesterday was New Years, so that'd make today, January 2."

"I know what the damn date is, Colby, I just ain't clear on the day. Is it six day, seven day, or what?"

"Huh, six day, seven day; what the hell are you talking about Riley?"

"That is his way of naming the days of the week. He don't use Monday or Tuesday, he uses numbers," Tyrell pointed out with a chuckle.

"There ain't nothing wrong with using numbers as days of the week- shit, there are seven days in a week, why not one day, two day and so on?"

Colby shook his head.

"Well, if my mind is clear, I'd say today is Saturday."

"So, six day?" Riley responded.

"Sure if you want to call it that. Uh-huh, today is six day."

"Okay, good now I'm clear. So today is six day, and you figure, Colby, that on two day next week we should be near the Columbia River?"

"We ride as hard as we did today, tomorrow, and I'd say we'd be damn close by Tuesday, yes sir."

"Three more days of hard riding, shit, why can't things be easier?" Riley complained.

He poured himself a coffee now that it was done, and draped his woolen blanket over his shoulders to chase away the cold wind that began to blow.

"Going to be a cold evening I think. Damn chilly already with that wind."

"January tends to be that way. We'll have to keep ourselves as warm as we can, I tell you though I certainly ain't looking forward to it. It is what it is though," Tyrell responded as he fumbled for his tin cup and poured himself a coffee.

"When Martin and I were heading to Willow Gate we got held up for a couple of days on a mountain summit. The wind up in those mountains was deafening. This here ain't so bad. It is cold though," Colby warmed his hands above the flames as he reminisced. "And to think we have at least three more months of this shit to live through."

"Thankfully, we ain't going to be out and about for those three months. Eventually we'll be back at the Fort and some normalcy," Tyrell said with hope and speculation.

"I guess that depends on how soon we can get this job over with. Who is to say we ain't going to be out on the trail for another three months?" Colby questioned.

"I say. There ain't no damn way I'm spending any more time on the trail after we settle this job. And if Ed expects us to, I'm going to tell him to shove it up his ass," Riley made clear.

Looking into the flames of their fire the three of them chuckled. It might have been cold and miserable, but the fact remained they were expected to do a job and that is exactly what they were going to do.

Black Dog who had taken off a few minutes earlier for a run or to chase a rabbit, returned with a torn up skunk or other small animal in his jaws, whatever it was it sure stunk.

The three men getting a whiff of what was dangling from the dog's mouth jumped up in a quick hurry and scooted off a distance. Black Dog quite content now lay down beside the fire and began eating the rancid smelling animal.

"Jesus, Black Dog, how about you take that elsewhere?" Tyrell questioned with anger. "C'mon, get the hell away from our fire."

Black Dog only looked up and as though he knew, exactly what he was doing and he continued to feast on the innards of the foul smelling critter. He wasn't moving.

"He ain't moving Travis," Colby said as they looked on.

"Nope, he ain't, damn dog anyway. We have two choices I reckon, we can join him and live with the stench, or we build us another fire here about somewhere."

"Let's gather some wood. There ain't no way I'm sitting beside that fire. No sir," Riley said as the three of them gathered wood and built another fire. As far as they were concerned, Black Dog could keep their first.

Once the second one was lit and shooting flames into the sky, the damn dog picked up what was left of his kill or find, and once more chased the men away from their second fire.

"Goddamn it! He's a rifle bit of center, Travis. Can't you get him to take that vermin elsewhere?"

"He's got a mind of his own Riley. I tried getting him to move along, he ain't listening."

"The other fire still has some flames to it, let's see if he'll stay here and we'll take back our first fire," Colby suggested.

In agreement, the three of them went back to their first fire. Luckily for them Black Dog stayed where he finally settled by the second fire.

"I can't believe that dog eats skunk or pine-martin, whatever the hell it is."

"Me neither, in all the years we've been together, I ain't ever seen him do that," Tyrell pointed out.

The musky scented air came in waves as the three of them settled in for the evening. It made for an unpleasant night's sleep, but tired, as they were it mattered little.

Early the next morning after biscuits and coffee, they were once more on the move.

"That damn dog stinks to high heaven, Travis," Riley said as they carried onward.

"He sure does. I reckon though in time it'll fade. Until then, we're going to have to tolerate it."

"Where the hell do you figure he found a damn skunk anyway?"

"I don't know Colby, likely dug him up from a den somewhere. I've never seen a skunk in winter, not sure they hibernate or not, and ain't even sure it was a skunk, all's I know is it stank to high heaven and ain't left the dog smelling to nicely either."

"I think they half hibernate and half don't," Riley added to the conversation.

Colby looked over to Riley and raised an eyebrow.

"Uh-huh, and what half hibernates, Riley?" Colby teased.

Riley only shook his head and chuckled, he wasn't even going to respond. Colby was certainly a witty bastard when he wanted to be.

At 10:00 a.m., they slowed their horses to a stop and took a few minutes to rest up. The sun was starting to warm things up by then, and they basked in the yellow glow.

"We're in for a nice day I think, should make traveling easy," Tyrell said as the three of them handed back and forth a canteen.

Rested now, they swung back onto their saddles and continued along the trail. The sun was indeed a nice change and it felt good shinning down on them. The snow covered branches of the cedars and pines that were along the trail and drooped with snow, sprung back as the snow fell from the branches as the sun continued to warm things up.

A short while later they came across a recent camp. They could tell by the number of hoof and footprints that four riders had stopped there and spent a night.

"As you said Riley, four riders were ahead of us and this here is the tell tale sign that you were correct," Colby said as they once more swung off their horses, and looked around.

"And look at this," Colby started as he pointed to the ground. "Those ain't boot prints."

Riley and Tyrell came over and looked at what Colby was studying.

"Nope, those ain't from boots- those are moccasins."

"Holy shit, you is right Travis. Looks like three men in boots and one fellow wearing moccasins, now what could that mean?"

"I think we know what that means, Riley. Means there is an Indian riding with three white men."

"Indeed it does, Colby, and they weren't here too long ago, two maybe three days ago."

"You two ain't thinking what I'm thinking are yous?"

"Chances are we is, Travis. I'd say we're either behind Atalmore's crew and the Apache Kid, or by some chance, there is a crew of four riding westerly that ain't Atalmore nor the Kid, and by some off chance one wears moccasins."

"Nope, coincidences like that are far and few between, I'd think. I'm betting it was Atalmore and his crew along with the Kid. They spent a night, maybe two here. That'd be my guess."

"Goddamn, Colby, you were jus' as right as I was. You're leading us right to them."

"Not quite, Riley, they're still ahead of us."

"Yes, they is, but I think we're tailing them. Even if they are a couple of days ahead, we keep following their trail and we'll catch up," Riley said, as he looked down the trail westerly.

Tyrell by now was leaning on his horse with a map in his hand.

"Looks like we're on this trail here," he said as the others approached.

He pointed at the map.

"If we are on this trail, there is a route which switches southerly about ten miles west of here. I say we mount up and head to those cross roads. Any sign of four riders heading south, we'd be certain then on whom we are following. I never thought it would be this damn easy, almost makes me wonder if we ain't in for a surprise."

"You mean like being bush-wacked?"

"Something like that."

"Atalmore ain't going to be waiting on us at all, he and the others are heading for Big Muddy, and they ain't going to stop until they get there. They'll be hard as hell to catch then, they could jump back and forth between the borders like a grasshopper from one blade of grass to the next," Colby said with sincerity.

"We'll have to see what comes of it as we carry on. If we can get close to them before they cross the U.S. border, we might have a chance."

"So, then, what the hell are we waiting for? C'mon let's get back on our horses and ride."

The three swung up onto their rides and continued at a slow gallop.

"You know Travis, we get this taken care of soon, the sooner we'll be headed back to the Fort, and that makes me a happy man," Riley pointed out as they heeled their horses and sped up.

They rode their horses hard for an hour or so, then once more slowed to a steady pace of cantering and galloping. Finally, they came to where the two roads split off. Indeed three riders it looked like headed south, there were no signs of a fourth rider.

"Shit, looks like three headed this way, there ain't no sign of a fourth, what the hell?"

"We must've lost the trail of the fourth along the way. Should we turn back and maybe have a slower look at things?"

"Hold on," Colby began as he swung off his horse. "Looks to me like a fourth rider has followed all right, 'cept he's using the hoof prints of another horse to cover his own damn tracks."

Tyrell and Riley trotted over to where Colby stood and they swung off their own steeds and looked on. Riley knelt down and looked closely at what Colby was talking about.

"Huh… Goddamn, I think you is right. So, there are four riders heading along this way, Travis."

"Looks like that don't it? Okay, so we'll carry on south from here."

Riley swung back onto his horse as did Tyrell, Colby though continued to look around, something wasn't right and he could feel it.

Tyrell pulled out his map again and looked at it.

"As far as I can tell, the U.S.A., border is still at least fifty maybe sixty miles south. Damn, could be they've made the border by now."

It was then the shot echoed in the distance, whizzing past Tyrell and knocking Riley clean off his horse. It was so quick and sudden, not even Black Dog had time to respond or warn of the impeding trouble about to take place.

"Son-of-a-bitch, I've been hit!" Riley stated as Colby quickly made his way over to him and helped him up off the ground and the two of them made for cover. Tyrell on the other hand remained on his horse and pulled out his rifle from the saddle sheath that held it and he quickly cocked it.

"How badly has he been hit, Colby?" Tyrell questioned with concern as he looked in all directions, trying to see if he could pin point where the shot came from. Unable to see anything he too jumped from his horse and made his way over to where Colby and Riley were tucked away in the bush.

Their horses scooted off into the trees, as Tyrell made the distance. He looked at Riley who was conscious but not in the best of shape.

"Jesus Christ, Riley, why the hell did you go and get yourself shot."

Riley inhaled deeply and looked at him.

"Didn't have much of a choice really, I don't reckon it is too bad. I still have all my faculties. I know what is what and what isn't," he said as he cocked his pistol and looked around. Colby too had his rifle ready as the three of them waited with trepidation at what was to come.

"I don't see a damn thing anywhere, why the hell aren't there more shots being fired, so that we could at least guess where the shots are coming from?"

"I reckon that ain't what this is all about, if whoever fired at us wanted to shoot more that'd be doing it by now. This was a way to slow us down. We must be damn close to someone that don't want us following," Tyrell said as he looked again at Riley, to make sure he was still breathing.

"You still with us Riley?"

"Am so, and I'm pissed off too, ruined my jacket and one of my best shirts. Jesus look at it a damn hole in them both and bloodstained. That really pisses me off."

Colby and Tyrell half chuckled. It was good to know Riley was his usual self. They waited a few minutes and when they felt it was all clear, Tyrell looked over Riley's wound.

The bullet had only grazed him, but had left enough damage that it would certainly slow the three of them down for the time being. Ripping away some material from an old pair of long underwear that he gathered from his saddlebags after they managed to get their horses back, he wrapped the material around Riley's ribs and using a stick, he twisted the tourniquet taunt.

"There that ought to slow the bleed down some," Tyrell gave the tourniquet one last twist and tied it off. Riley would be left with a finger size scare across his ribcage, but he would live to talk about it or return the favor to whomever it was that had ruined his shirt and jacket.

Chapter 7

Resting for a while longer before starting again, and making sure Riley was well enough to continue, the three men and Black Dog continued southerly, in the direction of the previous trail they were following.

Tyrell looked back at Riley who was lagging behind some.

"You doing all right back there Riley, or what?" he asked as he and Colby slowed their horses.

"I could be better, Travis, but I ain't dying, nor am I dead. Just, rehearsing everything that has taken place, and wondering why someone would shoot at us."

"Like I said Riley, whoever it was that fired that shot wasn't looking at killing us at least I don't think so, I think it was a way to slow us down and for the time being it has. It don't mean we ain't in the sights of the shooter right now at this present moment, so, quit your lollygagging and stick close to us."

Riley sped up his horse and caught up pulling in between both Tyrell's horse and Colby's.

"That better, Travis?"

Tyrell nodded.

"Damn right, I'd rather you stuck close for now, this way I can keep an eye on you and that wound of yours that ruined you jacket and shirt," Tyrell smirked he knew Riley was going to be fine.

"I'm still pissed off about the entire situation, so, don't be making jokes."

"Ah, come on Riley, we can always replace a damn jacket and shirt, but we ain't able to ever replace an old son-of-a-bitch like yourself. So from my perspective I'd rather see an old jacket and shirt with holes in them, than having to bury your old withered ass in the ground along some God forsaken trail that I assure you is froze solid, which would've made digging a real bitch," Colby piped up with a chuckle.

"I couldn't agree more." Tyrell said as the three of them continued onward.

"Hell, if I die, jus' string me up in a tree and let the buzzards have at me."

"Well, with the ground as frozen as it is, that is exactly what we would do, so if you don't want the buzzards eating out your eyes and pulling off your dangly parts, don't die."

"So yous would actually just string me up in a bloody tree if I die?"

"We'd come back in spring when the ground thaws some and bury whatever was left then."

"Jesus Christ, Colby, why the hell would we come back all this way for any bones that might be left?" Tyrell questioned with humor.

"Yeah, I suppose you is right," Colby replied as the two of them chuckled and shook their heads.

Riley didn't respond and he half chuckled himself.

Tem miles south, and crouching next to three decapitated corpses was Matt Crawford. He had also been on the trail of Barclay Atalmore and his Rebel Rangers going on five days. What he was looking at now wasn't what he had expected to find. He rolled one of the headless bodies onto their back, and searched through the pockets of the dead man looking for anything that might identify the bodies. With no heads attached or for that matter none visible to him, he wasn't sure if the corpses he was looking at were the three men he had been tracking.

Finding no identification on either of the dead men, Matt was at a loss of what to do next. Standing he scouted the area looking for clues on what might have taken place and who the men might be. In the distance along the bush line, something did catch his eye. He squinted and looked on. Something was definitely out of the ordinary.

Making his way over to his horse he removed his rifle and sighted in on the anomaly in the distance.

"Shit," he said in a low voice as he lowered his rifle. What he saw near the dark wooded area were three bodiless heads on pikes.

He couldn't tell from that distance what the men looked like, but his gut told him that they were the heads of Barclay Atalmore, Allan Webber, and Spence Hamilton, the Rebel Rangers he had been tracking.

Swinging up onto his horse he headed toward the bush line, the only way he'd ever know if his gut instincts were right, was to see with his own eyes up close that indeed it was Atalmore and his men.

The closer he got the more certain he was. It was a grotesque sight, three bodiless and frozen heads on pikes, and he wondered who in the hell might do such a thing.

Finally making the distance, he swung off his horse and walked the few steps to the first pike. Lifting the head up by the chin to see who the man might be, he shook his head in both remorse and dread.

"What the hell happened here Webber?" he questioned, now that he was certain who the dead men were.

With evening only a few hours away there wasn't much Matt could do, other than take the heads off the pikes and lay them on the ground next to the bodies. He covered them up with an old blanket. Then a short distance away set up his evening camp. It was going to be a long one. In the morning, he would reevaluate the situation and make appropriate plans on what to do next.

He was miles away from any town and the three horses the dead men had been riding were nowhere to be seen, or for that matter were there any tracks. The recent snowfall had obliterated any telltale signs on what direction they may have gone, or any other tracks that may have been there other than his own.

Sitting on his saddle near the small fire he had lit to take away the chill, he pulled out a note-pad, and wrote down his report on what he had come across, while, it was fresh in his mind and could be written in explicit detail. Pouring himself a coffee, he wrapped his hands around the tin cup to warm them, as he took his first swallow. His mind raced with what might have taken place and why. Nothing though made much sense.

Matt had been in contact with Ed back at the Fort, and as far as Ed knew Matt was supposed to be heading into the Yukon to take over security for Buck Ainsworth's hotel up that way, in the town of Mistyvale. This was to prevent Matt from being detained by U.S. Ranger Lee Griffith, who some weeks earlier had shown up in the Fort looking for Matt and to arrest him for crimes he had committed in the U.S.A., and to start the extradition process.

Ed though wasn't going to have any part in that and so he had given the Ranger little to no information on where Matt was or where he was heading, other than pointing out the fact that Matt was a law abiding citizen and now worked for McCoy's as a professional Private Investigations and Security officer. That was all Ed ever told him.

The McCoy's then came up with a plan to keep Matt away for as long as possible, until he became a Canadian citizen, and they sent him into the Yukon. Which is where Matt was supposed to be heading until by coincidence he heard about the escape of Barclay Atalmore and his two men, Allan Webber and Spence Hamilton all known members of the Rebel Rangers.

It was Matt's instincts and his knowledge on where the three escapees were heading, and so he changed his course and began to track them down, if not to apprehend them, than to see to it that they headed back onto U.S.A soil. Matt himself had once ran with the Rebel Rangers and although he had left the club- so to say, he never wanted to see them dead, but there they were, dead. How he would ever explain to Ed and the others that he had been tracking Atalmore, when he should've been heading north for his own protection and at the advice of Ed, was another story, but when the time came; he would.

His biggest concern now was what he was going to do with Atalmore and his men's mutilated bodies. He couldn't bury them, he didn't have the tools to build a skid to haul the bodies out and drop them off at the nearest town. He took co-ordinates with the compass he always carried and jotted them down in his note-pad along with the notes he had written, with the task done, he tucked it back in his saddlebag.

As darkness approached, he built up his fire to keep the chilly January evening at bay. He ate a can of beans although found it hard with each glance he made toward the mound of dead beneath his blanket. Tossing the half-eaten can onto the fire, he stood up and gathered more wood. He could see his own breath in the cold and clear evening air as he went about it. With enough wood now gathered for the evening, he wrapped himself up with his long felt duster and horse blanket then tilted his hat over his eyes.

Chapter 8

January 3rd 1892, with one last look at the blanket that covered up the dead men and before the first glint of sun poked over the eastern sky, Matt Crawford saddled up his horse and headed due north. There was nothing, he decided that he could do with the dead. He would report the incident to the first redcoat or RCMP detachment that he might come across.

The trail he knew where the bodies lie was travelled, and in time maybe someone else would discover them and report it long before he could. Still, he knew it was his duty to report the incident and he surely would the first chance he had, until then his goal was to make it to Mistyvale and the job that waited for him there.

Tyrell, Riley, and Colby were sitting around their morning fire waiting for their coffee to perk. It had been a cold evening and they huddled close to the flames.

"Goddamn, even this morning is cold. Ears almost froze off last night," Riley said as he looked into the flames and warmed his hands.

"Can't argue that point none and I don't reckon tonight will be any warmer."

Colby looked up to the sky.

"I think the day will be all right though, who knows maybe by dusk we'll be in some bow hick town where we can get ourselves out of the cold."

"Hate to break it to yous but we ain't going to be near any town by day's end. We might make the distance to Clear Water by tomorrow. Tonight though, we'll be out in the cold again." Tyrell now warmed his own hands above the fire.

Finally, the smell of coffee permeated the frosty morning air and they each poured themselves a cup.

"Well, here is to today and a damn warm bed to sleep in tomorrow night," Riley said as he raised his coffee in a cheer gesture.

When the sun brightened up the morning sky, the three of them gathered up their gear and continued on their way and the job at hand, to apprehend the Apache Kid and with luck chase down Atalmore and his Rebel Rangers at the same time, killing two birds with one stone seemed feasible.

"We best keep our wits about us as we carry on, whoever ruined Riley's jacket and shirt is still out there, and we don't know who or where they might be," Tyrell pointed out as they heeled their horses' flanks and sped up to a trot.

They travelled steady with only a few short breaks between to check up on Riley's wound. He was healing nicely considering the time that had passed since he had been shot, there were a few raw spots still but the rest had started to scab over and the little bit of seeping was to be expected.

"See told ya it weren't so bad. I think she's healing up nicely," Riley said as he laced up his shirt and tucked it back into his pants.

"I've had worse cuts to the tops of my feet, than that puny little wound to your side," Colby joked.

The truth was and each man knew it. Riley wasn't out of the dark yet. There was still the real possibility that an infection such as sepsis could take place, something that the aged were unable to fight off easily without medical attention, the onset could take a few days but if it happened, Riley, would be in trouble.

"As long as I don't see no puss I ain't going to make a fuss," Riley rhymed as to save each of them from the worry.

"Making up rhymes don't change the situation Riley. You could still get an infection, and we ain't going to be able to doctor you none out here."

"Hell, I'll pour some whisky over the damn wound if comes down to that, Travis. No need to worry about that. I've always healed up nicely," Riley said with a smile.

"Yeah, well I suppose you'd know better than I, but, you start getting a fever or start feeling sickly, you better damn well tell me, or I'll kick you so hard in the backside when I find out, that you'll cough up your balls."

"Trust me, I feel any of those things, you'll be the first to know as to save myself the embarrassment of coughing up my balls. Jesus, couldn't you have been least wise a bit cordial when you said that?"

"The cordiality goes in the wind if you start feeling sick and don't tell me."

By mid-day, the sun had warmed things up, and they were only a few miles away from where Barclay Atalmore's body along with the bodies of the Rebel Rangers that rode with him now lie covered up by an old U.S.A Ranger issued woolen blanket. Black Dog took on the scent of the dead as they drew closer. His peculiar demeanor alerted Tyrell, that something wasn't right.

Tyrell slowed his horse down to a stop, as did the others.

"What is going on Travis?" Colby asked he pulled up next to him and looked in the same direction, followed by Riley who asked the same.

"Ain't sure, Black Dog seems to have picked up a scent of one thing or another or he's spotted something. I don't see a damn thing and I ain't a hound so I don't smell a damn thing either, Black Dog though… he does," Tyrell replied with confidence and certainty as the three of them continued scouting the area.

"We best make a formation of sort, Riley since you is wounded you need to pull that steed in between Colby and me. Colby make sure that rifle of yours is ready, I'll make sure mine is too," Tyrell said as he pulled it from his saddle sheath and loaded it.

"What about me, what am I supposed to do?"

"You think you could shoot?"

"Damn right I can shoot," Riley made clear.

"Well then if we need to do any shooting, shoot," Tyrell looked at him and smiled.

"Goddamn right I will. Now let's get and see what that dog of yours seems to think is ahead. I'm ready."

Heeling their horse the three of them carried onward, their eyes and ears alerted to every sound and sight. At the top of a little knoll and to the right of trail they could see that there had been a recent fire, it was what they saw next that turned what was a half decent day into grisly one.

"What the hell do we have here?" Colby mentioned as he made his way over to the blanket-covered mound. Flipping the blanket off with the barrel of his rifle, he stepped back in shock, as did both Riley and Tyrell.

"Their heads is clean off, Jesus Christ, what the hell," Colby stated as he looked again.

"Hold on," there was a short pause, as Colby looked closer. "Shit, these here is Atalmore, Webber, and Hamilton."

"What!" Exclaimed Tyrell and Riley in unison as they stepped closer and had a second look themselves.

"These is Atalmore, Webber, and Hamilton, I can assure you of that," Colby repeated with sincerity, shock, and horror.

"Who the hell would've done that to them and why?" Riley questioned, as he now agreed with Colby that the dead men were no other than Barclay Atalmore, Allan

Webber and Spence Hamilton, the Rebel Rangers they had been tracking.

Colby only shook his head he had no answers.

Tyrell knelt down and looked at the bodies, he himself wasn't certain if the dead were that of Atalmore and his Rebel Rangers, but he could certainly tell that, the men had been dead for some time.

"I can tell you they've been dead for a while, their flesh is froze solid, makes them dead for at least two maybe three days," Tyrell said as he now stood up and tossed the blanket back over them.

"You certain they're Atalmore and his crew?"

"Damn right, their faces might be frozen, but I know it is them, can't ever forget the faces of what once might have been family."

"Goddamn, this kind of ruins my day. As law enforcement agents of sort it is our duty to bring them in or in the least report it and let the provincial law deal with it."

"How are we supposed to do that? There ain't no other horses around here that we could tie their asses to."

Tyrell scratched his chin as he contemplated, "Nope there certainly ain't, but, we are required to follow the laws of the land. It needs to be reported Colby, it is as simple as that."

Riley never said much, he was looking around for clues on what might have taken place. He noted that one rider headed north and by the look of the tracks, they weren't as old as the bodies, the tracks were fresh and likely from that morning. Next, he looked at the old blanket that covered the bodies, and took note of the 'Property of U.S.A., Public Safety', insignia woven into the top of the blanket with gold and red thread, it was faded and worn, but he knew what it read.

"This is a bloody U.S.A Public Safety issued Ranger blanket."

It didn't seem to be that important since the dead men were all once U.S.A. Rangers, however it seemed odd. The dead men had escaped a Canadian prison. Where would they have gotten the blanket, and why was there only one?

"Can you remember Colby if either of these dead men had a blanket like that?"

"I can't be sure of that Riley. I never looked at any of their bedrolls in the time that I ran with them. If I were to make a guess, I'd say no."

"Well then, I'd say whoever found them or did this to them at one time or another was an officer of the U.S.A Public Safety. You can't pick these up from the local merchant. That much I know. I also know that early this morning one rider headed north of here."

"I noticed those tracks too," Tyrell sucked on an eyetooth, as he looked northerly. "It ain't the direction I would expect the Apache Kid to travel."

"Who is to say it was him that left here?" Colby questioned, as he looked around trying to make sense of it himself.

"No one can say that, but, if what we have suspected that the Kid was trying to catch up to them or meet them in Big Muddy or for that matter riding with them this whole time, then logic would dictate that he would have witnessed what happened or he's a suspect, which at the present time can't be denied."

"I suppose the Kid could've done this, but he ain't the one that covered them up. What if, it was that Ranger fellow that showed up at McCoy's, looking for Matt? Let's say he was trying to track Matt down and happened upon this by coincidence. It would explain the blanket and the one horse leaving the area northerly."

"Could be that is how it is, in which case, I would assume he'd report it. So we're still left with a dilemma, what the hell do we do?"

"I can tell you the tracks left by the horse and rider that left this place ain't the Kid's, the horse hooves are too big for an Indian pony, and the rider wore boots that are about a size too big, for Ski-be-nan-ted, I'm sure jus' like all Apache's he has small feet."

Colby interjected in mid conversation as Tyrell and Riley bickered about this, that, and the other thing as they too tried to make sense of what it was they came upon.

Colby's observation took both of them by surprise.

"What, you don't know if Atalmore or any of the others had a Public Safety issued woolen blanket, but you know the size of an Apache's feet?"

"I know Apache feet are small, Indian ponies also have a small hoof print, these tracks here, they're too big for either. Never cared what Atalmore or anyone else ever wrapped their selves up with."

Colby looked up to Tyrell straight-faced, he was serious and knew what he was talking about, regarding both the rider and the horse that left there.

"I'm sorry Colby, I didn't mean to sound uninterested in what you observed. I'm a bit edgy I guess finding these headless men and such. I do think you are right about the rider and horse, that don't mean the Kid didn't do this, and like Riley points out maybe someone else passed by and did the right thing by covering them up. It is still a Goddamn mess that we have to deal with."

The three of them grew silent as they contemplated what next to do.

Riley spoke first.

"In conclusion of the ghastly scene we're looking at, we can't just stand here and think about what it is we have to do next. Let's get settled for the evening. It is too late now to go traipsing off after the rider that left here, or to try to make it to a town of some sort to report this. We can decide on what, when, and where to go from here come morning."

Riley grabbed his horse by the reins and led him over to where the recent fire had been. He tethered him to a sapling and unloaded his gear. Tyrell and Colby both followed behind him and tethering their horses, they went about setting up for the evening.

"I feel a little uneasy setting up camp so damn close to those I once knew who are now without heads," Colby said as he sat down next to the fire and looked again at the mound covered by a blanket.

"I ain't too cozy about either. Nevertheless, we have to stay put for now, to guard the dead from vermin so that no other parts and pieces are torn away. Come morning we'll decide what next to do."

Tyrell reached over to his saddlebags and pulled out the map. Looking at it from the light of the fire, he could see that there was a small township ten or so miles west.

"There is a town not far from here, if I'm looking at the terrain and mountains correctly. It is about ten miles west of here, called Sanction Creek. I'm guessing it is likely a small town, probably a mining town. There should be some kind of law near there or maybe even a telegraph office. Might even be a doctor so they could take a look at your wound Riley and add some salve or something to it."

"Doctor, shit, I don't need no doctor Travis, I ain't in no pain, and she's stopped leaking."

Riley brought his tin cup to his lips and took a swallow of the freshly brewed coffee.

"Besides until this gets cleaned up. It is our moral duty to protect the dead from uncertain further mutilation, from the wolves and such. What we need to do is this," Riley started as he looked around, "one of us has to head west, and the others need to stay put, to keep the vermin away. A ten-mile return trip can't take longer than a day. Once we get this mess out of the way, we can concentrate our efforts in tracking down the Kid, now that we know what has become of Atalmore. We can say our problems although not the prettiest of outcomes, are less one now."

"I don't know where you learned your math, Riley, but it also added a couple of problems and has slowed us down. I'd say we have three problems now. One is we don't know what happened here, two, we don't know who ruined your shirt, and three, we must've lost the Kid's trail back there somewhere," Tyrell gestured with his chin.

"Whoever we decide stays back in the morning will have to try and find that trail again. Let's hope it don't snow, 'cause that would add a fourth problem."

"What about who it was that left here? There is our fourth problem. Ain't we going to go after them?" Colby questioned.

"The law can do that. We ain't got the time nor do I want to make it our fourth problem. We report it to the law, give them our evaluation, and point them northerly. We already know that the rider who headed north ain't the Kid, so there ain't much point in changing the direction we've been tracking him," Tyrell responded as he looked back the way they came.

Back there somewhere he knew they would find the Kid's trail once more. What seemed to bother him more than any of the three problems they had, was problem two; *who had shot at them and why?*

Chapter 9

It had been a fitful night of sleep for the three of them. Tyrell was the first to rise that morning and without a morning coffee or a biscuit, he and Black Dog headed west to Sanction Creek guided only by the early morning glow of the slowly disappearing moon.

It wasn't as cold as it had been on previous mornings, which made traveling along the imperfect trail not as bad as it could have been. He was nonetheless glad it hadn't snowed. His mind drifted as any man's would in such peace and serenity. The silence of the morn took a turn as he heard in the distance the oncoming sound of a rider. He slowed his horse down, commanded Black Dog to alert and guard, and made himself ready for any unwanted encounter. Ready now as he would ever be, he slowly trudged on.

The approaching rider and himself locked eyes a short while later. For all he could tell the approaching rider was simply that an approaching rider. Black Dog showed no aggression and so Tyrell relaxed his pistol grip and continued.

By now, the two riders were close enough to share a few words.

"Howdy," Tyrell said first as he nodded and slowed his horse to a stop, it wasn't uncommon for travelers on lonely trails to greet each other.

"Hello back. Wasn't expecting to see anyone 'long this trail."

"Nope, nope, me neither," Tyrell responded.

The man reached around to his saddlebags and pulled out a wanted poster. Tyrell at first thought the man was reaching for perhaps a gun and his pistol hand quickly grasped the butt of his .45.

Realizing now that wasn't the case Tyrell once more relaxed. The man pulled up his horse close and unrolled the poster.

"You ever seen a man that looks like this?" the rider asked.

Tyrell looked closely at the battered wanted poster.

He hadn't seen anyone who looked like that.

"Can't say as I have. You must be a lawman?"

"No sir, the man I'm looking for is my brother. I need to find him before the law does."

The rider rolled the poster back up and tucked it away again in his saddlebags.

"Well, mister," he began as he turned his steed, "if you ever do see a man that looks like that, stay clear of him, he's a cold blooded killer and makes quick work of those he kills," and with that the rider began to trot away.

Tyrell called after him to hold up.

"Hold up a minute there, mister."

The rider slowed his horse and turned back.

"What is it?"

"About five miles up ahead are two men, they're friends of mine. My name is Travis, the three of us work for McCoy's Private Investigations and Security," Tyrell said as he showed the man his credentials.

"We came across three of the four men we've been tracking yesterday, they're dead, and their heads are clean off their shoulders. The day before that one of us took a bullet. Does that sound like something your brother might do?"

The man lowered his head in both dread and shame. Looking back up to Tyrell, he sighed and inhaled deeply.

"It is hard to say what Alvin might do, to be honest, Travis, it was, right?" the man asked.

Tyrell nodded.

"To be honest Travis, I want to find him before the law so I can end him."

Tyrell interjected before than man said anything more.

"Are you saying you want to kill your brother? That is probably something you don't want to say to a law enforcer."

"Whether you are a lawman or not, that is exactly what my intentions are. Alvin has been on the run for more than two weeks, he murdered his way out of the mental hospital where the law sent him three years ago, after he escaped from the first one he was sent to. The law finds him before I do; they'll toss him back in, simple as that. They say what Alvin suffers from is schizophrenia. The law looks at that as a sickness, and he can't be hung or put to death because of it. Now does that make any sense to you?"

Tyrell was at a loss for words. He wasn't sure how to respond.

"No, I don't suppose it does make a lot of sense. But, that is the law," he finally suggested.

"Law or not, it doesn't make it right. Alvin won't stop killing, even if they put him back inside, he'll escape again. We warned the judges and prosecutors a longtime ago, about Alvin, they didn't listen then, and they ain't listened since."

The man explained in few details how Alvin at age twelve started torturing and killing family pets, burned homesteads to the ground, and killed several men and women before the law finally took him in, and classified him as insane.

"Now you know," the man finished.

"Jesus, I can't imagine a family having to go through all that, and I can understand your reasoning on what your intent is. I ain't going to try and stop you. I only wish you'd let the law deal with it."

"Nope, not this time. This time I'll bury my brother."

The man turned his steed, "thanks for letting me know about your friends up ahead, I'll be sure to tell them I saw you."

"Before you leave, can you tell me how close I am to Sanction Creek?"

"The only thing at Sanction Creek is a riverboat landing of which I crossed over on this morning. I reckon you are looking for a redcoat to report the dead you and your friends found. The closest town that has any law is fifty miles west of Sanction Creek. You could head southwest to Fort Shepherd, or Clear Water, both about twenty and twenty-five miles southerly, there are usually men dressed in red tunics protecting the border along that way somewhere. You can't get to Fort Shepherd due west the way you're travelling now, without a few days ride."

Tyrell shook his head.

"Damn, well then I guess I'll head back to the others, you don't mind me travelling back the way I came alongside you do you?"

"Not at all," the man said as Tyrell caught up and the two carried on.

"You never did tell me your name," Tyrell mentioned as they sauntered onward.

"Nope, I sure didn't."

Tyrell waved his hand through the air.

"Probably best that way, since I know what it is you are settled on doing."

"Trust me it isn't something I'm looking forward to. I do know though it is something that needs doing."

Silence enveloped the two as they continued heading easterly. Black Dog biting at their horses heels.

It was Riley, who noticed the two riders approaching. He stood up from the fire and looked on.

"Look at that Colby, looks like Travis has found us a lawman."

"Shit, that didn't take him long at all. Good, we can get on with it and find the Kid now," Colby said as he took a swig from the tin cup in his hand.

Finally, Tyrell and the man riding with him made the distance and the two swung off their horses.

"Been told by this fella, Sanction Creek don't have no lawmen, got to head to Clear Water or Fort Shepherd."

The man riding with Tyrell only nodded his acknowledgement of both Riley and Colby, and then made his way over to where the mound of dead were covered up. He pulled back the blanket and looked on, then with a heavy sigh covered the bodies back up.

"I'd say this was Alvin's handy work, I'm surprised he didn't put them on pikes, he likes to do that."

"What, who the hell is Alvin?" Riley questioned.

The man walked over to the fire and warmed his hands.

"Alvin is my brother, escaped the asylum a couple weeks ago. Been on a killing spree since."

"Hold on, you're saying your brother did this?"

"Chances are, yep."

"Who the hell are you?" Colby asked the man, he was as confused as Riley. Here was a man whom they thought was a lawman telling them that his brother was likely the killer of Atalmore and the others.

"My name don't matter much, but, I'll tell you this. The man that did these killings here, I'd say was my brother."

Tyrell looked over to both Colby and Riley and shook his head, the man hadn't even told him his name, he had no idea who he was, except for the fact that he had a brother named Alvin who was an escaped mental patient.

With his hands warmed up and time slipping away, the man stood up from the fire and swung back onto his horse.

"I'll be seeing yous," he said as he tilted his hat and continued easterly in search of his brother.

"What the hell, Travis, who was that guy?"

"I don't have any inclination, never mentioned his name to me. All I know is that he is looking for his brother. He's going to kill him. That is all I know Riley."

"He admitted to you that he's going to kill his brother?"

"That is exactly what he told me."

"We can't let him get away with that, if he freely admitted what his intent is, we ought to stop him."

Tyrell shook his head.

"I don't see much point in that Riley. His brother is a cold-blooded killer. He has escaped a number of times each time he is brought back in; he's tossed back into the asylum. The families of the dead he left behind saw no justice for those crimes and murders he committed. The law can't hang him 'cause he's mentally unstable and that is looked upon as an illness, and although that is the law, sometimes the law don't make a lick of sense."

"So, we're just going to let him kill his own brother?"

"Look what his brother has done to Atalmore and the others, and if we didn't know the killer was an escaped mental patient and we tracked him down, would we bring him in or shoot him?" Tyrell questioned.

"Likely shoot him," Colby spoke out.

"There you have it, Riley. We don't know nothing about the man, or his brother, 'cept what was told to me, and that is, his brother is named Alvin. He is an escaped mental patient with a thirst for killing, now I ain't about to go traipsing after a man who knows more about the killer than we do. And I ain't about to stop him."

"Well, Jesus, I don't know Travis, it don't seem right to me," Riley pointed out.

"Right or wrong, if we don't know anything about what has happened here, then we're in as much of the dark as we were yesterday."

"But, we ain't are we? We know the name of the man that may be responsible, and we know the man's brother is looking to kill him. It don't sit right in my gut at all."

"Forget about it Riley, shit, we don't need no more headaches. I say we report the dead as we first planned, we don't have to mention anything else to any lawman, other than what it is we found. That is how I see it," Colby said as he crouched down and poured himself another coffee.

"I agree with Colby, Riley. We don't need to say a damn thing about anything, other than the fact that we found Barclay Atalmore and his men with no heads. That is all we got to say."

"I don't know, Travis. It don't seem right," Riley looked into the flames of the fire and shook his head.

"It could be also Riley that it was Alvin that shot at us the other day and ruined your shirt and jacket, and had we seen where the shot came from, we'd have shot back, wouldn't we have?"

Riley nodded.

"Yeah, I suppose you is right on that account. The thing is we wouldn't have known what it is we know now about the possible shooter. It makes it different now."

"No it don't, Riley. If it was, Alvin and we had a clear shot on him we would have shot him regardless. If the son-of-a-bitch popped out of the woods right now and began shooting at us, we'd shoot back and we'd be shooting to kill. Whether we knew or didn't know his mental state."

"Well then, there ain't no point in trying to make heads or tails out of the situation, other than what it is we are faced with. Clear Water is about a twenty five mile ride, and I reckon one of us can make the distance before it gets dark, but, they ain't going to make it back before tomorrow, and that would put us a day behind on our other obligations.

I say we head that way together. Find a redcoat and give them the rundown on what we found. We leave this mess behind us, and carry on with what our objective is now that we ain't got to pay much attention on the whereabouts of Atalmore; and that is to pick up the trail of the Kid," Riley responded.

Although the entire situation still didn't sit well with him, he knew the others were probably right. Besides there was no point in arguing about something that already seemed to have been decided. They'd keep their lips shut about what they knew about Alvin and his brother's will to kill him.

"Makes sense to me," Tyrell responded as he added what was left of the wood that had been gathered to the fire. It would keep it burning for a few hours after they were gone, it would also help mark the spot even if it snowed, and keep vermin away until it burned out.

"That being settled, I say we get saddled up and head to Clear Water," Colby said as he began gathering his gear and saddling his horse.

Riley did the same and the three of them headed southwest toward Clear Water, leaving behind the grisly murders they had stumbled upon. *It was what it was.*

It was 8:00 p.m., when they made it to Clear Water. They had travelled hard and steady all day long, to make the distance. It wasn't a big town, no towns in the area really were, but there was indeed a redcoat.

"There is a lobster back now," Colby gestured with his chin as they rode into town. They pulled their horses to a halt next to where the redcoat was standing.

"Something I can help you men with?" the constable questioned as he noticed their intent to stop their horses in front of him.

"Indeed there is. My name is Travis Sweet, this here is Riley Scott and Colby Christian, we work for McCoy's Private Investigations and Security out of Fort Macleod," Tyrell said as he introduced himself and the others.

"Uh-huh and…?" The constable questioned as though he cared.

"Well, sir, we were asked by the Governing law of Canada to apprehend and detain Barclay Atalmore and his men, whom of which I'm sure an officer of the law, as yourself, is aware, escaped from the Calgary minimum security penitentiary some weeks ago," Tyrell began now that he had the constable's undaunted attention.

"I'm aware of their escape, yes. What of it? I can tell you they haven't been seen around here, or they'd be in the city cells," the constable responded with arrogant confidence.

Tyrell smirked at the constable's arrogance.

"I'm sure they would be, sir. The thing is we found the three of them about twenty-five miles northeasterly, their heads clean off their shoulders, covered up with an old U.S.A. Department of Public Safety blanket yesterday, I'd say they're apprehended."

The constable was now showing more of an interest.

"Decapitated, you mean?" he asked with shock.

"Yes sir."

"How do you know it is them, if they haven't any heads?"

"Oh, their heads were there all right, just not on their shoulders, and if your next question is, 'how can we be sure' that it is them, I can tell you we were tracking them and their trail led to where they lay now. I will also mention I was one of the men that brought them in. I know what they look like. The faces on the heads are that of Barclay Atalmore, Allan Webber, and Spence Hamilton,"

Tyrell said as to protect Colby's relationship with the Rebel Rangers.

Colby was the one that identified them and although at first Tyrell wasn't sure, he was now, as all the evidence pointed to their identities, and he did notice the similarities to how he remembered they looked in life.

"You say they are covered up by a U.S.A. Public Safety blanket?"

"That is correct. That is how we found them."

"Goddamn, all right well, you folks are going have to follow me and fill in a report and show me your credentials and whatnot."

"By all means, lead the way," Tyrell said as they followed the constable toward a small building with an outside cell.

"Welcome to Clear Water R.C.M.P detachment," the constable said as the three of them tethered their horses, and stepped inside.

The constable gestured for them to sit as he fetched a report log.

"I'll need to see your credentials and any other identification you might have," he started as Tyrell and Riley produced their credentials. He looked over to Colby expecting to see something from him, but Tyrell interjected.

"He works for Riley and I, and has taken the oath, ain't got no credentials yet, but we vouch for him and so does Ed McCoy, Lieutenant Bob Cannon and Special Constable Rick Bash, of the Fort's detachment."

The constable accepted the explanation and proceeded to write down what he had already been told about Barclay Atalmore and those that rode with him.

"Here is what I got so far. The three of you work for McCoy's Private Investigations and Security. Your names are Travis Sweet, Riley Scott, and Colby Christian. You were trailing Barclay Atalmore and those that escaped with him from the Calgary minimum security prison down east. The three of you stumbled upon the bodies of three dead men, who have been decapitated, and have been identified by you, Travis, as Atalmore, Webber and Hamilton," he stopped there as he took a breath, "Jesus, quite thing isn't it?"

"It is. You forgot a couple of things though, they is covered up with an old U.S.A. Public Safety blanket. They're also laying 'bout twenty-five miles east of here along the trail that heads to Sanction Creek, you can't miss them, they is sprawled out near the trail," Colby pointed out.

"Oh, yes, right." the constable said as he jotted that down too. "Well, here is what I got so far, here have a read and sign your names," he handed the report over to Tyrell who read through it.

In agreement with what the constable wrote out, he signed his name, as did both Riley and Colby. Handing the report back to the constable, he asked if there was anything else.

"I reckon you have it all there, is there anything else you need from us? We still have other business to tend to," Tyrell asserted. "By the way who should we say we reported this too?"

"No, there is nothing more that I need. Not at the moment, I have your names though and know where you work. If we need anything else you'll be notified, and I am Constable Joe Hallard," the constable pulled his heavy jacket to the side to show his name tag pinned to his red tunic.

"All right, well I guess that is it," Tyrell and the others stood up. "Is there by chance a telegraph office around here?"

"There is but it is closed by now, it opens at 6:00 a.m."

"Okay, looks like the three of us will enjoy some Clear Water hospitality then."

"By all means, the hotel has rooms and meals. Enjoy your stay." The constable said as the three of them exited. They grabbed rooms at the hotel and a hot meal and then turned in for the evening. It was nice to sleep in a bed for a change and not under the cold clear skies of January.

Chapter 10

By 7:00 a.m., the next morning on January 5 they had sent a telegram off to McCoy's to let Ed know what had transpired with Atalmore and whom they reported it too. Then with one last coffee from the hotel restaurant, they set off once more in search of the Apache Kid.

"It is two day today ain't it?" Riley questioned as they rode out of town.

"Yep, Tuesday, all day Riley," Tyrell responded as they carried on.

"So, by Colby's calculations from the other day we should be getting close if not already near the Columbia and the U.S border, but since we was sidetracked a day, we still have another two days ride, damn."

"It ain't that bad, we don't need to worry no more about Atalmore, only thing we need to concentrate on now is finding the Kid."

"The thing is Colby, we can't be certain if the Kid even went that way, since we lost his trail."

"Nope can't even be certain if the fourth rider that was tailing Atalmore and crew was the Kid, not no more. Could be it was that Alvin fella. I know the Kid a bit, as I've said and I know where he's likely heading and it is to Big Muddy. He'd be safe there, and could live in those hills for a long time without being noticed," Colby pointed out, "we got the Columbia River to make, and from there the Casino Mountain's once we get there, it is only a short distance to Big Muddy," he added.

"Tracking the Kid is all about luck now, ain't it?" Riley complained as much as questioned.

"It was always about luck, Riley."

"Yeah, I suppose you is right, Travis. When we were tracking Atalmore though it seemed like we were on the right track, and that the Kid was travelling with them. Can't say that now."

"There are a lot of things we can't say now. Could be the Alvin thing is a coincidence, could be it ain't."

"It is like we're back to square one then isn't it?"

"Indeed it is Riley, indeed it is."

Ed and Brady McCoy were sitting in the backroom of the McCoy's office having coffee when Buz the telegrapher showed up.

"Ed, Brady," he said loudly from the front counter. It was odd not see one or both of them approach as soon as the front doors opened, he realized then the reason was that the front bell was taken down.

"Ed, Brady," he called again. Finally, Ed approached.

"Morning Buz, what you have for us?"

"Got a telegram here from Travis, sent from Clear Water, that is quite the distance west, Ed."

"Yeah, he and Riley and our newest and youngest employee Colby, are on assignment up that way," Ed mentioned casually as he took the folded piece of paper from Buz. It took a few seconds to read it, and he hollered for Brady. Brady came out of the backroom a coffee in his hand.

"What is it old man?" he asked as he met him at the front counter.

"We can scratch Atalmore and the others off our wanted list," he said as he handed Brady the telegram.

Brady's jaw drop when he read it.

"Shit, they found them headless," he said in both shock and surprise. "Who would do a thing like that?" he questioned as he looked up to Ed.

Ed only shrugged.

"I ain't got a clue. Travis says they reported it to a constable Hallard up in Clear Water."

"I know old man, I can read, it is a damn curious thing ain't it?"

"It is," he looked over to Buz, "thanks for bringing this to us Buz."

"No problem Ed, you folks sending back a reply?"

"Nope, we don't know where to send one. Travis said they're leaving Clear Water, but didn't tell us where the hell they are going."

"All right, well, I guess I'll head back," Buz said as he ducked out of the McCoy's office.

"Jesus, quite the thing isn't it, old man, Atalmore and the others losing their heads," Brady half chuckled.

"Makes a man wonder what went on."

"It sure does. But the telegram clearly states what went on, someone took off their heads."

"You don't sound remorseful, Brady?"

"Why would I be remorseful? They was wanted felons."

"Maybe remorseful is the wrong word, you don't seem bothered by it."

"I am a bit. Shit, it is a curious thing as I said earlier. But, you live by the sword, you die by it, ain't that an old proverb, or something."

"It is, and I'm surprised you know it," Ed teased with a smile.

"I paid attention to the preachers as I grew up, I ain't deft old man."

They were getting the Atalmore folder together when Buz returned for a second time with another telegram, this one from Matt Crawford.

"Got another one here Ed, it comes from Midway," he handed it to Ed.

"Huh, well things have become two fold more curious now, Brady."

Brady approached and Ed handed him the telegram.

"Say's here Matt found the same thing. What the hell. Ain't he supposed to be heading to the Yukon by now?"

Both Ed and Brady were now quite dumbfounded. Neither knew what to think.

"I haven't a damn clue what is going on. At least Matt gave us some co-ordinates, but, it ain't going to do us no good," Ed ran his fingers through his hair as he contemplated.

"I guess you won't be sending back a reply?"

"No, Buz we won't be."

Buz nodded and once more exited.

"I'm trying to make sense of this. If Travis and the others stumbled upon the same thing as Matt, what the hell was Matt doing that far west?" Ed tried to put things into perspective.

Brady took a sip from his coffee as he leaned up against the front counter.

"I ain't got no answer old man. Both telegrams come from different places. Midway is northerly, and Clear Water is westerly. Could they have been travelling together, and tracking down Atalmore and the others when they came upon the mess? Then they split up? This whole thing is off the wall."

"I guess for now we ain't really got any answers one way or the other."

"More questions than answers I reckon."

"What even seems more odd is there ain't no mention about the Apache Kid, whom, Travis and the others were supposed to be tracking down. Damn," Ed shook his head. It was going to be one of those days, where everything made sense until one thing didn't, and from there the day turned to shit and apprehension.

"I think I have an idea on what might have happened. Say, Matt came across Atalmore and the others, or saw them from a distance and decided to head after them, he loses their trail along the way and when he finally comes across it again, he finds the three of them dead. There ain't much Matt could do, so he takes co-ordinates, jots down what he has found and heads north.

Next, Travis and the others are also tracking Atalmore, they're a day or so behind, and coming from the opposite direction, low and behold they stumble upon the same mayhem. Matt by now has already vacated and there ain't no sign of him, so, Travis and the others do their diligence and report it to the law in Clear Water. From there they continue west, toward the Columbia River, and destination unknown, but likely Big Muddy, still in search of the Kid."

"Goddamn, that does make some sense, Brady. Could be that is how it was. Humph, never once thought it through like that."

"That is why I get paid the big bucks," Brady chuckled, although his analogy made sense, there wasn't any proof in the pudding, it was all conjecture.

"Well, I guess we wait now and see if anything else comes through the wire. I like what you said though, Brady. I guess your mama never raised no fool," Ed smirked.

"That she did not old man."

Having ridden for near four hours, the three riders slowed their horses to a halt near a frozen waterfall. It ran over the bank and under an old bridge, they had to cross.

"I don't know, Travis, that snow covered bridge don't look safe to me," Riley mentioned as the three of them swung off their horses and looked on.

"I reckon it is safe, Riley, folks use it all the time when travelling this way I assume."

"It don't look like it's been crossed in a while, there ain't no tracks coming or going."

"Let's tether the horses and go have a closer look on foot, could be we'll have to cross one at a time if things don't look good," Colby suggested as they found trees to tether their rides.

Making the distance the three of them looked the bridge over, and walked it, kicking snow out of the way, as they did to assure there were no rotten logs that could break or fall through. Standing on the other side, they looked back.

"I'd say as long as we lead the horses and stay where we just walked, things will be all right."

"I reckon, yep. We'll cross one at a time," Riley pointed out.

They rested a short while back the way they came near their horses. Then one by one traipsed across. Tyrell and his horse along with Black Dog crossed first, followed by Colby and then Riley. Only thing was Riley's horse didn't want to cross. He fought with the horse, as it reared up and snorted, pulling Riley right back the way he came.

"Goddamn, stupid horse! You're going to be food for the damn wolves if you don't stop with this shit! Now c'mon let's try this again."

The second attempt wasn't any different than the first and once again, Riley found himself back on the wrong side of the bridge.

"Jesus Christ, I don't know what has got into him, Travis. But, I don't think this mule of a horse is going to cross that bridge."

"What if I meet you halfway, maybe that horse of yours is a bit snow blinded."

"He ain't snow blinded, he's jus' being a Goddamn asshole."

"Hang on Riley; don't give yourself a damn heart attack." Tyrell said, as he handed his horse's reins over to Colby and began to walk back. He had made it about halfway when something caught his eye. He stopped dead in his tracks and looked over the side of the bridge. Frozen into the ice was the body of a man. "I think I know now what has been scaring your horse Riley," Tyrell said as he crept closer to the side of the bridge being careful with every step he took.

"And what the hell would that be?" Riley questioned still clenching his horse's reins.

"From what it looks like, I'd say there is a dead man frozen solid in the creek," he stepped closer to the side to get a better view, "correction, there is a dead man froze solid in the creek," he added as he now had a better view.

"How come that dog of yours never picked up on that?"

"The horse I reckon is a lot taller, Riley, the dog can't scent things frozen in water, nor is he tall enough to look over the edge. I reckon your horse spotted it and it spooked him."

"Well, why the hell did it have to be my horse?" Riley questioned as he looked to the sky above.

Tyrell chuckled and shook his head.

By now Colby had tethered their two horses and was standing next to Tyrell and looking on at the dead man.

"I'd say he's dead. Must've fallen over the side or something."

"I reckon, or he floated down from above the water fall."

"What the hell are we going to do Travis?" Riley questioned impatiently, "I still need to get my horse across to the other side."

"Maybe with Colby and I standing here, your horse ain't going to see what's been spooking him. Try again." That was all he had to offer.

"All right, I guess that is all we can do," Riley said as he and his horse began to cross again. This time the horse crossed. Riley sighed in relief as he tethered him and made his way back to where Tyrell and Colby stood Black Dog at their sides.

"Shit, everyone keeps throwing rocks at us, don't they? What the hell are we going to do about this pleasant surprise?"

"I ain't sure there is a damn thing we can do about it. Swinging an axe to chop him out increases the risk of one of us getting pulled under."

"So, we mark the spot, take note of the location and let the law know in the next town, that is about all we can do ain't it?" Riley questioned as much as stated.

Tyrell contemplated for a moment, he knew what had to be done.

"Nope, we're going to have to chop him out, by the time any law made it here the creek might be in full runoff, and that body is going to swim with the fish to only God knows where."

"I'll get a rope and the axe," Colby said, he knew exactly what was going to be needed.

"I can't believe we're going to chop him out, Travis. It ain't going to be me swinging no axe."

"That is all right, I'll do it. We'll tie off the rope somewhere or you and Colby can hold onto it. I'll tie it around my waist and do what I can to break him out of there. The ice breaks though, you and Colby better be damn fast at pulling me out, I ain't too akin to getting hypothermia."

"Maybe Colby ought to do it he's lighter than you or I?"

"Nah, he's a bit green still I think Riley."

"The hell I am," Colby said as he approached with the axe and rope. "I'd do it."

"I'd rather you and Riley stay up here, if I get tired of chopping, we can switch."

"All right, but don't be thinking I'm green and couldn't do it, 'cause I know damn well that I could."

"I knew you was close when I said that Colby, I was only funning with you. Now, I'm going to head over the bank and make my way down there. When I get there toss me the rope."

Tyrell turned and walked back across the bridge and began making his way to the frozen creek. Once out of earshot, Colby spoke to Riley.

"Here, hang onto this rope," he handed it to Riley who stood there confused as Colby crossed the bridge himself and grabbed another rope from his horse. Making his way back, he smirked.

"Watch this," he said with a chuckle as Tyrell finally made it to the edge of the creek below the bridge.

"You got that roped tied off up there?"

"Sure do, Travis, yep."

"Okay toss it to me."

Colby tossed him the rope. Tyrell took a second glance as the rope landed in its entirety beside him. He looked up to see both Riley and Colby laughing.

"Well, you said toss me the rope. Sorry about that Travis, I didn't have her tied off as I thought, I must be green still."

"Yeah, yeah, enough with the damn jokes, you better have another rope up there tied off or I'm going to kick your ass." Tyrell hollered from below as he chuckled and shook his head.

"Here you go," Riley responded with a smile as he tossed him the rope. Tyrell gave it a few tugs to make sure it was tied off. He looked up to the others as he tied it around his waist.

"All right here I go," he said as he stepped out onto the ice doing his best to keep his balance and not slip and slide all over the place, the rope helped some. Finally, he knelt down and slid across on his knees.

The first swing of the axe caused the surface to crack in all different directions like a spider web. Still it held his weight and he slowly chipped away, it took near an hour but he was able to expose the man's shoulders and was able to get the other rope Colby tossed him tied around them, everything below his chest though remained in ice. Soaking wet and cold from the water that now began to spread across the ice, made it even slicker and more perilous for him to be standing on it. There was no way he was going to chop any more of it away. He made a final judgment then to get off the ice as quickly as possible, stumbling and crawling in a heated rush as he went.

"You all right Travis?" Riley shouted as Tyrell made the creeks edge.

"Yeah, I'm all right, almost went for a cold swim though, and damn it, I don't know how to swim," Tyrell hollered back.

By now, Colby had made his way down to where Tyrell rested and tossed a blanket over him.

"You don't know how to swim, yet, you'd attempt a damn thing such as that which might require you to swim. You're crazy, Travis, you know that."

"Least now we got a rope around the man's shoulders, can tie that rope around a tree or something, it'll keep it from floating downstream when the creek thaws. We'll do like Riley suggested earlier, we'll let the law know."

"Seeing what could have happened, I reckon we should've done that in the first place."

"By the time the law would've got here Colby, there is a good chance that body would've floated downstream. That would leave the next of kin with no answers on where their loved one might be. We did what we had to do Colby."

"I blame Riley's horse, that is all I got to say," Colby took the end of the one rope and tied it around a tree.

"There, that ain't moving without being untied. C'mon, let me help you up the bank, you must be damn frozen."

Colby helped Tyrell up the bank and over to where Riley had started to get a fire going.

"We should have flames in a few minutes, Travis. Keep that blanket wrapped around you and strip out of those wet clothes. Colby, grab the coffee fixing's, and dry clothes out of Travis' saddlebags."

"Already on it Riley."

Flames from the fire began to warm things up. In drier clothes now, Tyrell was feeling good. His boots were drying on sticks and his feet were up on log near the fire that Colby dug out and rolled over. They drank coffee and reminisced for about an hour, and things were finally calmed down and back to normal.

"You don't suppose that fella in the drink is the Kid do you Travis?"

"Hard to say Riley, I know the body's head has dark hair, his face though is pretty much distorted, and froze in a peculiar way, it weren't a very pretty sight, I'll tell you that. The only way we'd know for sure is to chop the rest of the body out and have a look, but it ain't safe to do that. I reckon it'll remain a mystery to us."

"I don't think it is Ski-be-nan-ted, shit that body froze up in that creek has got to have been there for some time. It didn't jus' freeze up like that in two or three days. That would take time I would think."

"It would Colby, yes sir, still it'll always be a mystery to us, 'cause I ain't about to waste anymore time in proven it one way or the other, by chopping out the body," Tyrell inhaled deeply. "I reckon we should get going," he checked to make sure his boots were at least dry enough to wear.

They were.

"We've rested long enough and I'm dry and warm. No use sitting when we still have a distance to go," he said as he slipped them on.

In agreement, the three of them swung back on their horses and continued west.

Chapter 11

The evening of January 5, they had made the distance to another wagon trail that headed southerly. The signpost read Columbia River outpost 15 miles.

"We're getting closer to the Columbia River, fifteen miles to go," Riley pointed out.

"Yeah, another days ride. I say we find a place to set up for the evening, not much point in carrying on. We start off in the morning again and we'll make the outpost by late afternoon," Tyrell responded.

Riley pointed to a small clearing a short distance away. "Right there I reckon will do."

Satisfied with the spot they dismounted and set up for the evening. It didn't take long before their fire was cooking up coffee, beans and biscuits. They fed their horses a few handfuls of grain as they waited for their own meals.

"We sure have seen a lot of shit in these past few days eh, Travis?" Colby questioned as he pat his horse and looked southerly.

"There ain't no denying that, we sure have. Makes a man wonder about things don't it."

The three of them now turned heel and made their way back to the fire and the coffee that was now brewed. Tyrell poured each of them a cup and handed them off.

Riley nodded his thanks as he took his cup and gently blew on it.

"You know, in all the years I've been in this business, not once have I ever saw a man with no head, and in one moment I see three, and later on we find another froze in the water. I tell ya's both, times ain't what they used to be."

"The chances that you'll ever see a man with no head again, Riley, is pretty slim. It ain't like it is going to be a regular daily occurrence. I don't think I could even handle that, and I'm a few years younger than yourself," Tyrell looked into the flames of the fire, "can only imagine what it does to an old folk," he half chuckled.

"Old or not, it likely does the same thing to the young, and that is it don't leave a very pretty picture bouncing 'round in our heads."

"Jesus, Riley, you must've grown soft since we found that mangled tore up body of Gabe Roy," Colby teased.

"I knew what to expect when we went looking for him. This here thing with Atalmore and the others caught me off guard. I ain't been able to shake it from my mind yet."

Riley took a sip from the tin cup in his hand as he gazed into the flames.

"I'm too old to remember much of the past, but, I don't think I'll ever forget the look of surprise and fear that was froze on their faces," he continued his gaze into the fire.

"You're lucky Riley you only have three pictures bouncing around in your head. I have four," Tyrell said solemnly.

Colby crossed his arms as he sat on his saddle near the fire, and shook his head.

"I don't know why either of yous feel that way, but, I can tell you, it don't make a lick of sense to me. You both sound like babies. Shit, think about it. Yous are in the business certainly not so much for the money, since there ain't ever much to be got on bounties, but for each of your needs to be a bit on the wild side. Coming across Atalmore and the others in a sense is a damn good thing, they was hindering our search for the Kid. Which, we still ain't found. Hell, there could be even more death around the next bend for all we know, going soft now before…"

Tyrell interjected.

"Going soft? Hell no, I ain't going soft Colby. I am just trying to make sense of it. How come you haven't any ill feeling about it? You knew each of them a hell of a lot better than Riley or me."

"Sure, I did know them, and I feel a bit of remorse on what became of them, but, I also know that means there is a man running 'round that has murder on his hands, and another man that we was requested to find and detain. The dead is dead, and whoever did it to them ain't. The man we need to find now to fulfill our obligation to whomever it was that hired us to find him still needs to be found."

"It was the Police Commissioner that requested McCoy's service, and yeah, you are right we do need to fulfill our obligation and we certainly will, but in the meantime it don't hurt none to reminisce about what it is we came across," Riley pointed out.

"That is the problem, yous keep thinking about it."

Both Tyrell and Riley nodded in unison, Colby was right. They needed to concentrate their efforts in finding the Apache Kid everything else was all history and there wasn't a damn thing they could do about the deaths of Atalmore, and his crew, nor the death of the man they found froze in the creek. They had done their part, had reported the death of Atalmore, Webber, and Hamilton to the authorities, as for the frozen man, they'd report that incident too, the first chance they got.

It was late afternoon on January 6, when they finally made the distance to the Columbia River outpost. There was a riverboat landing, a small livery stable a pint size general store, and a few small houses scattered here and there. That was it; that was all. There was nothing else, not even a Mounted Police station house.

They pulled their horses to a stop in front of the general store and dismounted, tethering their rides to the horse pole.

"Not much here," Riley spoke as they made their way inside.

The man behind the counter smiled at them as they approached.

"Afternoon gentlemen, is there anything I can help you with?"

"Yeah, when is the next river boat due?" Tyrell asked as they stepped closer.

"Last one today has come and gone already. The next won't be here until mid morn tomorrow."

"Damn it. Is there a place where we can stay?"

"You could try the livery-stable it'll keep yous out of the cold leastwise."

"There is no hotel or rooming house where we could get rooms and a meal nearby is there?" Riley now asked. He wasn't looking forward to spending a night in a goddamn livery stable.

"A day's ride east of here there is," the man replied.

"Well now, that don't help us none does it, if we want to catch that boat in the morn?"

The man shrugged.

"Sorry mister, but that is all there is."

"All right. I guess we'll head over to the stable and see what we can come up with."

Tyrell wrapped his knuckles on the counter and looked at both Riley and Colby, and shrugged.

"There ain't much more we can do about the lack of rooms. The stable will keep the frost off us, c'mon, let's get."

Thanking the clerk the three of them saddled up and made their way to the livery stable.

The young man that ran the place met them and they introduced themselves.

"Uh-huh, and so, yous is looking for a place to stay?"

"Was told by the store clerk we might be able to spend the night here, since there ain't no other place but east of here."

"I can afford yous one of the rooms, I suppose. I got six horse stalls and two small rooms. The horses keep for the night is a dollar. The rooms each have a woodstove, bunk bed and table. Two of yous is going to have to sleep on the floor. I'll let yous have the room for three dollars."

"All right, we'll take it."

Tyrell reached into his pocket and fetched a few coins that added up to the four dollar cost, and he handed it to the stable master, who took it and led them to the back of the stable.

"Here is where yous can stay, it is mostly used by summer help, and the odd drunk river boat captain. Since this ain't summer and there ain't no drunken riverboat captain nearby, I don't mind making a few bucks every now again from offering it up to passers-by," he said as he opened a door and gestured for them to make themselves comfortable.

"Yous can cook on the stove and fetch water from the back well if yous like. I'll get your horses settled and tend to their needs," the man nodded and exited.

The three of them looked around. It wasn't anything special other than their dire need to stay out of the cold winter nights as much as possible, it was far better than sleeping under the stars again.

"A little bit cramped, but we got a table, a bunk bed and a cooking stove. Nothing wrong with this set-up at all," Riley said as he pulled up to the table and sat down.

Colby made his way over to the shutters and opened them, the view was westerly and looked out across the Columbia River.

"Got a view of the Columbia, can almost see clear to the other side," he said as he turned back and sat across from Riley on a piece of stove wood. Tyrell spent a few moments getting the fire lit as they settled in.

"There that takes care of that, should get toasty warm in here soon."

He grabbed the coffee pot from their gear to fetch water from the well out back. Looking around he could hear the sloshing from the Columbia River as it caressed the sandy rock covered shore nearby. Black Dog pranced over to him and sat down. The two of them stood there in the company of each other looking west and listened. Soon the sun would be behind the mountains and another dark and cold evening would be upon them.

"We'll be on a boat come morning Black Dog, it is going to take us to the other side and from there I hope we can pick-up on the Apache Kid's trail, otherwise this has been a waste of our time."

Tyrell squinted as a cold wind pierced his eyes.

"C'mon Black Dog let's get inside, you staying with the horses or are you going to grace us with your presence tonight?" Tyrell questioned as though the dog would answer, and in his own way, he did, when he followed him into the small room and found a spot to lie down near the wood stove.

Adding coffee grinds to the pot Tyrell, set it on the stove to perk.

"Going to be getting dark in a couple hours, I think we might get snow tonight."

"I hope not. The Casino mountains are going to be treacherous enough with the lil' bit we have already," Colby pointed out.

Riley who had stretched his legs out was cleaning his fingernails with the small knife he had for that purpose as Tyrell pulled up a bale of straw that was against the one wall and tossing his horse blanket over that, sat down. The three of them sat in self-contemplation as the small room slowly filled with the scent of freshly brewed coffee. Colby brought the pot over and set it on the table.

"We got any fixings to add to this coffee? Or is we drinking it black?"

"I reckon we got some sugar left."

Riley stood up and put his knife away as he dug through his saddlebags, producing a half tin of sugar and three cans of beans. He set the sugar down and opened the beans, not bothering with a pot he set the cans on the stove to warm up.

"All right so we got beans a cooking, coffee already brewed and it ain't even dark yet. Too bad this place ain't got no entertainment, the two of yous want to play some cards?" he asked as he sat back down and poured himself a coffee.

"It would help kill some time. Sure, I'm up for a few hands of stud. What about you Colby?"

"Deal the cards, Riley, I'm in. What is going to be the wager? Cards ain't no fun without a wager," Colby responded.

"Any money we have, Colby is all for gear and supplies."

"The wager don't have to be for money, Riley, how about we play for the bunk-bed, whoever wins three hands gets it. The losers sleep on the floor and make coffee and biscuits in the morning," Colby challenged.

Tyrell chuckled.

"That sounds fair to me."

"All right, I'll agree to that wager, too," Riley reached into his shirt pocket and pulled out a deck of cards. They cut for deal. Colby drew the high card, and so he dealt the first hand.

Riley won the first and second hand, Tyrell the next and Colby like Riley won two in a row. He shuffled the cards, cut the deck, and made the deal. It was cut and chase between he and Riley. Whichever of the two won that hand, would sleep comfortably on the bunk bed and the mattress it contained. There were actually a few tense moments as the two of them smiled and taunted each other.

Tyrell though knew he had already won that hand and so he sat confidently silent, smirking. He managed to pull a two pair hand of nines and sixes on the first draw. He didn't even bother taking cards on the second. Now he watched as each Colby and Riley pondered their moves. *How many cards would each toss down if any?*

"Dealer takes one," Colby said as he tossed one card down and looked over to Riley.

"How many you going to toss up there, Riley?"

"Ain't sure I need any jus' yet Colby, give me a minute to think about it," Riley looked at his one ace, his nine, his four, seven, and the jack. If he were playing for money at that point he'd toss his four and seven away and hope on getting another nine, ace, or jack. He finished eating his beans as he contemplated.

"All right, I'll take two," Riley tossed his two lowest cards to the table, and Colby dealt him two new ones.

"And you, Travis, how many?"

"None for me Colby, I'm happy with what I got."

"There ain't no more draws after this one, Travis."

"I know. I'm fine with what I got. I guess I call it."

Colby took his card and looked at his hand, then flipped them onto the table.

"Two pair, threes and eights," he looked over to Riley who flipped up his Ace high.

Colby chuckled, "not a very impressive hand there Mr. Scott."

"It's been a while since I played stud," Riley complained thinking it was over for him and the floor would be his bed.

Colby now averted his attention to Tyrell.

"So, what you got there Travis?"

Tyrell smiled and flipped his cards up.

"Two pair, sixes, and nines. I think that beats you, mister, Christian."

"Shit," Colby said as he slid the cards over to Tyrell to deal.

"I think we is all tied up here, next winner wins the bunk-bed," Tyrell teased. He didn't care who won, neither of them did, it was all just fun and games, something to do to pass the time.

"Just deal the damn cards Travis."

"Got to let me shuffle them up, Riley, be patient."

Tyrell shuffled them a few times, cut the deck, and dealt out the hands.

In the end, it was he and Riley that would end up sleeping on the floor. Colby had managed, the *'Dead man's hand'* which consisted of black aces and eights and the queen of diamonds. Although neither of the men had never paid much attention to the curse, legend, or were superstitious in any way, for a moment the room grew deathly still as they looked at Colby's laid out hand and what the significance if any it meant.

"Damn, never drew a hand like that before," Colby said with shock.

"Ah, don't worry about it Colby, that stuff about the dead man's hand is all poppy-cock."

"No, I mean aces and eights. I don't care much about their colors. I ain't ever drawn them together in stud, not once, ever."

"Well, you did tonight. The bed is yours you won it fair and square," Riley tilted his hat to acknowledge the win.

"Damn right I did and I'll sleep on it to," Colby said with a grin as he grabbed the cards and put them back into the deck. He would of course let Riley have the bunk when the time came, he was old, had a bit of a wound and the cold wooden floor Colby knew wouldn't do Riley any favors, he would be better off on the bunk and would save he Travis from Riley's unrelenting belly-aching as they slept.

"The card playing killed a couple of hours leastwise, another cup of coffee or two and I reckon we should lay out our bedrolls, morning comes quick and we need to keep our eyes opened for the riverboat," Riley said as he poured himself another coffee and offered up a pour to the others.

"Yeah, fill mine up Riley," Tyrell slid his cup over and Riley filled it.

"What about you Colby, you want the last of it?"

"Might as well, them beans we ate need to be washed down with something."

"I thought they was good beans, warmed up in the can like they was should've even made them better. It sure helps with the clean up."

Riley poured the last of the coffee into Colby's tin cup.

"That can I ate had that big piece of pork fat in the bottom that always kind of makes me a bit queasy. The coffee will fix that up. Thank you Riley," Colby took back his tin cup and took a swallow.

The evening proceeded and they continued conversing for a while longer until their coffees were finished. Finally, tired and anxious about what the next day might bring Colby gave the bunk bed up to Riley, and sprawled out his bedroll on the floor alongside Tyrell and Black Dog.

"You sure you want me to take the bunk, Colby? You won it fair and square."

"I don't reckon the floor will do you any favors, besides you have that wound and you're old," Colby chuckled, "nope I want you to have the bunk, Riley. The floor suites me fine."

"Well I ain't 'bout to turn it down for a second time," Riley smirked like a kid in a candy store as he laid out his bedding on the bunk and sat down on it. "Damn, going to sleep like a lamb tonight," he said as he removed his boots and stretched out.

"I hear any of that hellish snoring tonight Riley and I'm going to put a pillow over your face," Colby joked as he kicked off his boots and lay down, tilting his hat over his eyes.

"There are two things a man learns quickly in this business, Colby. One, men snore, two is beans give men the vapors. I'd be more worried about my flatulence than my goddamn snoring. G'dnight," Riley rolled over and smiled.

Although it was a bit of a distasteful conversation, it brought on a rebuttal from Colby, as was expected.

"You just keep those blankets wrapped up around yourself. I've got used to the wafting smell of horse shit, coming from the stable don't need you adding to it."

"What makes you think that is horse shit you smell?" Riley teased.

"Jesus, if it is you that stinks like that, you might have something wrong with you. If it is simple old age, then goddamn, I don't want to grow old."

Tyrell who was lying on the floor wrapped up in his own blanket, chuckled as the two went back and forth. He had nothing to say or add. With a few more retorts and snickers from both Colby and Riley, all fell silent as the three of them drifted into sleep.

Chapter 12

U.S.A. Ranger Lee Griffith by coincidence that morning of January 7 was also awaiting the riverboat scheduled to land at the Columbia River outpost. He was as unaware that three of McCoy's men were also at the outpost, as the three of them were unaware of his presence.

For the past few months, he had been trying to track down Matt unsuccessfully of course. He was now heading back to the United States emptied handed. He wasn't at all sad about the way things had turned out, nor was he happy.

Matt Crawford was still a wanted felon by the U.S.A Department of Public Safety, and it had been his job to find him and begin the extradition process, but alas, that isn't how things turned out. The more he tried to learn about Matt's whereabouts the less he knew.

It didn't help his cause any that Matt Crawford had been found not guilty of crimes he committed in Canada, or for that matter that he was now working for a Private Investigations and Security outfit known as McCoy's.

It didn't help his cause any that Matt was good at disappearing he always had been, nor did it help his cause that Matt was protected by judicial law and the laws that governed Canada. By no means was Ranger Lee Griffith defeated, in time he knew, he and Matt Crawford would be eye to eye. For now though, he would report his meager findings and come spring he would once more be on the prowl for Matt Crawford. That was his due diligence and duty, and he had never relinquished on a duty.

By now, Tyrell, Riley, and Colby were beginning to stir. Gathering up their bedrolls and gear, they prepared for the next lag of their journey, not before coffee and biscuits though. That now out of the way they exited the small room and made their way to their horses.

"Good morning gentlemen. How was the room last night?" the stable man questioned as he met them.

"It worked out well, kept us out of the cold. We thank you for the use of it," Tyrell said as he and the others haltered and saddled their horses.

"It was a cold one last night, the water troughs even froze up."

"I reckoned it was going to be a cold one. Only stepped outside once to gather water and the wind was cold, I figured we'd have seen snow."

"Nope, didn't snow, froze is all."

"Well, that is a blessing," Tyrell proclaimed as he swung up onto his horse.

"The riverboat should be landing soon, I guess I'll be seeing you folks around. You ever get back this way you know where you can stay."

"Thanks for the invite, and you can bet if we ever come back this way, we'll pay the fee again."

"Good. All right happy trails," the man said as he stepped away and watched as the three of them rode toward the riverboat landing.

They were surprised to see another rider waiting on the boat too, and they casually made their way to where the man and horse stood. The man looked at them and nodded. They returned the gesture and smiled.

"Morning mister. You waiting on the boat too?"

"That'd be the only reason I'd be sitting here on my horse," came his reply in a southern drawl.

"Where are you heading?" Colby questioned as to be polite and to strike up a conversation, there was something about the way the man talked that that made Colby curious.

Tyrell who noted the five-point star peeking out from the man's heavy felt jacket, questioned him.

"You are a U.S. Ranger aren't you?"

"I am. My name is Lee Griffith, and yours?"

"Well Jesus Christ, you're that U.S. Ranger that was snooping around McCoy's some time back ain't ya?" Riley spoke out.

"Perhaps, but neither of you have answered my question. Who are you?"

"I'm Riley Scott, the three of us work for Ed McCoy."

"Uh-huh, so you are Riley Scott, I guess that makes one of you Travis Sweet. I know all about your employment with Mr. McCoy. Are you waiting on Matt Crawford by chance?"

"No sir. Matt as you know is on assignment."

"That I do know Mr. Scott, and I don't suppose you're going to indulge me on where that might be?"

"We ain't at liberty to indulge such information. You being a lawman ought to know that."

"What I know about the laws and what lawmen do for one another are two different things. Most are cordial to one another, and give helping hands. Your type though, Private Investigators and the like, live by a different set of rules."

"Our type and the like, you are certainly an arrogant son-of-a-bitch, ain't you Lee?" Colby blurted out.

Lee Griffith chuckled.

"I didn't think Travis Sweet was such a young man, you are he aren't you?"

"No sir he ain't, I'm Travis. This is Colby Christian."

"I see. I know a little bit about him too," Lee averted his eyes to the approaching riverboat that they could see.

"What the hell do you know about me?" Colby questioned.

"I know you were picked up along with Barclay Atalmore, Allan Webber and Spence Hamilton, last summer, I know you were sentenced to twenty days of community service for your part in trying to gain access to Matt Crawford's credentials and warrants for his arrest.

I can assure you hadn't you been implicated it that minor crime and hadn't already been sentenced for it, I'd arrest you right now, and take you back to the United States. What I don't understand is what it is you are doing in the company of so called 'Investigators' that are required to uphold laws."

"Hold on a second, you can't threaten him with that, Ranger Griffith, and it is none of your business why he is in our presence," Tyrell communicated with distain.

"It isn't a threat. I'm clearly telling him how it would be. I'll also point out that if neither of you want to be implicated in obstructing justice, by keeping Matt Crawford's whereabouts and agenda away from me, to say nothing further. I'm not here to communicate with lesser lawmen."

Lee Griffith heeled his horses flank as he moved a few paces closer to the landing riverboat.

"Did you hear that, 'lesser lawmen', he called us, who the hell is he to say that to us?" Riley questioned with disbelief.

"Jus', a goddamn yokel from yank land," Colby said.

Lee Griffith hearing the comment turned his head slightly acknowledging that he had heard the remark, but he did nothing. His tired eyes now looked at the riverboat as it docked and he watched as a few passengers stepped off. Then given the signal to board by the riverboat captain, he boarded followed closely behind by McCoy's men.

Nothing was said between the four passengers as the boat lurched forward. The captain slowly increased the speed of the steam driven paddle wheel that pushed the big boat, it stuttered and coughed a couple of times before the sailing turned from rough to tolerable.

The captain finally spoke.

"These old steam driven paddle boats sometimes give us trouble, she won't sink though," he assured above the loud churning of the sixteen-foot deep paddle wheel.

He looked ahead as he turned the wheel and pointed the bow toward a point along the far shore of the Columbia.

"It'll take near twenty minutes to get across, providing the wind don't pick up."

"What happens if the wind picks up?" Riley questioned with trepidation and concern.

"It'd slow us down some, and we'd likely end up a few miles downstream," the captain responded as he once more gave the wheel a turn. "No problem though," he continued, "the boat would battle its way back up, there ain't never been a boat lost between here and the other side. Up river, though where the Columbia and Kootenay rivers meet is another story. We're in one of the calmer river corridors, down this way the current ain't so tough. There is always a first time though that one might go down, let's hope today isn't that day," he threw in for a chuckle.

"To be honest, Captain, that don't make me feel any better."

"You ain't been on many boats, barges or ferries have you?"

"Nope, I sure haven't and I ain't been on many steel rails either, don't like them, and I ain't so sure I feel any better about riverboats or water crossings. Land bridges and bridges in general I get, never had any reason to use the rails or the boats."

"The world is a big place now mister, lots of places to see and countless adventures await all men and women that have an inclination to use the riverboats and rails. Times are changing," the captain, pointed out, as he stepped below deck and tossed a few shovels full of coal into the steam engine.

Riley almost pissed himself with no man at the helm.

"Jesus Christ, he just left the goddamn wheel," he exclaimed as he held onto his horse and grasped the wooden railing hanging on for dear life.

Tyrell chuckled.

"Settle down, Riley. He's tossing more coal into the engine, he'll be back."

"Yeah, well how the hell do we know the damn boat is heading in the right direction. Jesus Christ, he's been gone about an hour already."

It was of course an over exaggeration, he had only been gone a few short minutes.

Finally, the captain reappeared and took his place at the helm, making sure their coordinates were true. He reached into his pocket, pulled out a flask of whisky and waved Riley over.

"I reckon you might want a swig of this, mister."

"Damn right," Riley reached for the flask and took a long swallow, then wiped his mouth with his sleeve. "That was a damn life saver. I needed that I tell you."

The captain smiled, pleased that he was able to calm the old codger down.

"I figured you might have needed a drink. Glad it helped you some. Where are you folks coming from? If you don't mind me asking."

"No, that is fine, we're from Fort Macleod."

"That is quite the distance away, you must be lawmen. I swear there is a convention of you folks gathering somewhere."

"What makes you think we is lawmen?"

"The badge that friend of yours wears tells me that story."

Riley snickered.

"Shit that fella ain't riding with the three of us. He is a lawman though, a U.S. Ranger, goes by the name of Lee Griffith he's a bit of an ass too I might admit. Nope he ain't riding with us. You said there seems to be mass of lawmen running around, what did you mean by that?"

"Those fellas that stepped off before yous boarded, were special constables of the Royal Canadian Mounted Police, from what I gathered, have come this way to retrieve the bodies of three dead escaped convicts.

I think I overheard them say, they escaped from a Calgary prison. I assume since one of yous that boarded is wearing a badge that you was all lawmen yourselves. Didn't realize the one with the badge was a U.S. Ranger, don't see many of those around here."

"This here is a unique situation Captain, the three of us work for McCoy's Investigations and Security, it was us that reported the bodies. I'm sure surprised to see it being handled so quickly."

The captain's interest grew.

"So you are all lawmen after all?"

Riley nodded.

"Like I say a unique situation."

"It sure is. I wondered why the four of you ain't spoke to one another. I think I get it now."

"Yeah, the ranger is an ass and didn't speak to kindly to us whilst we waited for you to dock."

"You have any inclination on why a U.S. Ranger would be in these parts?" The captain was curious he didn't care either way.

"Can't say as I do, you'd think he'd be riding alongside the Mounties that off loaded on the other side, and would help them retrieve and identify the bodies of the three U.S.

escaped convicts. The man is blind though to that incident, don't think he even knows."

Riley chuckled.

"He's supposed to be one of America's finest."

"Ain't lawmen obligated by some oath to relay information between agencies and whatnot?"

"It ain't a requirement by any means. It is called cordiality and respect. If neither is giving, neither is returned. Rest assured, we'll tell him once we get a few hours up the trail some, it seems we're heading in the same direction."

"You three must be the ones I heard tale that were looking for that escaped lunatic Alvin."

Riley raised an eyebrow and shook his head.

"We ain't looking for anyone named Alvin, I can tell you that."

"I guess it don't matter much why yous would be heading south," the captain said as he muffled the engine's air intake so he could gently coast onto the shore. Not trying to be rude, he had to concentrate on landing the big stern wheeler.

"Anyway, mister, we're about to dock in two minutes, it's been nice talking shit with you, I hope you enjoyed your first river crossing by boat."

Riley nodded his appreciation to the captain for striking up a conversation with him and keeping his head cool as they made the distance to where they now docked.

"All right, folks, you can off load now," the captain, said as he lowered the bridge onto the landing dock.

He nodded at each of them as they stepped off. The four of them now a safe distance away, he brought up the bridge, put the old stern wheeler in reverse. Then, he slowly turned the big boat around, and once more for the second time that day, headed to the opposite side to meet any other passengers that may be waiting.

It was his daily routine, five trips a day back and forth. Humdrum at times and other times interesting like the first trip that morning had been. It was no wonder why riverboat captains were a wealth of information. Folks either stuck to themselves or mingled and talked with other passengers, a lot of the time these things could be over heard, or the captain was spoken to directly. Information about this, that, and the other thing, were often learned, on the decks of riverboats.

"You and the riverboat captain, Riley, seemed cozy, what was yous talking about?" Colby questioned as the three of them watched the riverboat gently course its way back to the other side.

"I think he was trying to keep me calm for the most part, never showed much interest in what we talked about. I did learn a few things though," Riley said now that Lee Griffith was out of earshot.

"Oh what might that be?" Tyrell asked.

"Those folks that stepped off on the other side when the riverboat landed were special constables of the Mounted Police, heading to Clear Water and Sanction Creek to retrieve the bodies of Atalmore and the others, and I reckon to investigate their deaths further."

"Well goddamn, that was quick on their part. I didn't expect it to be that soon."

"There's more, he thought the three of us were looking for that Alvin, fella. He seemed to know about that fellas escape. Heard tale he said that three men was looking for him. I guess he pegged us to be those men."

"You didn't tell him why we was here did you Riley?"

"Nope, he didn't seem to care one way or the other. I was more interested in hearing what he had to say. He figured the four of us was riding together. Spotted Griffith's badge right from the start and assumed we was all lawmen from the same brand. He seemed surprise when I told him Griffith was a U.S. Ranger.”

“You figure he would have noted an Apache if one were to have crossed on his boat?” Tyrell put forth.

“I reckon he would’ve, I didn’t even think to ask since I was choosing my words careful as to not give too much information away, especially with that Ranger on board.”

“Maybe we ought to stay put and wait for him to make his way back, we could ask him then.”

“I don’t know Colby, might not be any passengers on that side, and I ain’t sure how the riverboat system works, if the captains and their vessels stay put for a certain amount of time and wait, or if they simply turn back around.”

Colby turned in his saddle and looked behind to where they had last seen Lee Griffith.

“Shit, looks like our friend the Ranger has moved on, don’t see him anywhere.”

Turning his horse, he sauntered over to where the Ranger last was, and he looked for tracks to see which direction he might have gone. Tyrell and Riley watched as Colby looked on, then he trotted back.

“The Ranger didn’t head south as we suspected he would, nope, turned up river westerly.”

“Wonder why he’d do that?”

“Your guess is as good as mine, Travis. I have no clue.”

“Since Lee ain’t near, I suppose waiting on the river boats return ain’t such a bad idea now.”

“I’d agree, let’s get out of the wind though.”

Tyrell gestured to a windbreak of tall standing cedar.

“Right over there would suffice.”

In agreement, the three riders ducked behind the cedars, dismounted, and tethered their horses. From where they were, they could watch for the boat’s return in relative comfort with no wind blasting them. It was still cold, but not nearly as cold as it would have been had they simply waited on the barren shore.

"Quite the curious thing, that Ranger heading westerly, ain't it?" Riley stated as they continued their gaze of the Columbia and waited.

"Let's have a look at my map, it might detail something up westerly," Tyrell reached into his saddlebags and retrieved the map. Looking at it, he noted there was another outpost about ten miles west. It was likely where Lee headed, maybe to retrieve supplies.

"Looks like there is another outpost up river, likely has a general store, could be Lee headed that way for that reason."

"Why would he do that if Fort Shepherd is only a hop, skip and jump away, and leads into the U.S.?"

"Well, I don't know, Riley. Only Lee knows the answer to that. Nonetheless, once we speak with the riverboat captain, and he don't have anything to share regarding our questions we'll still head south. If the Kid is heading to Big Muddy, we might get lucky.

He'll need to cross the Columbia and I reckon the Salmon River the same as we're going to have to, one way or the other to do that, or, has already done so. To cut straight easterly would plant him in the Rocky Mountains, and at this time of year, it would certainly add days to the journey. The southerly route, right along the two borders at this time of year makes a lot more sense. Once he gets to Idaho, he'll head to Flathead and straight northeasterly from there right back into Canada and Big Muddy. That sound about right Colby?"

"Not too far off at all Travis, we stick close to the border and continue due east. Near Fort Peck in Montana or there about, we head north, right back into Canada and to Big Muddy. It took us a week's ride once we made the U.S. border when I was running with the Rebel Rangers. It was an easy ride over the flatlands, a hell of a lot quicker than passing through the Canadian Rocky Mountains even at that time of the year. Ain't sure how things will be in winter though."

"It turns out we have to continue southerly, I guess we'll soon find out," Tyrell said as they finally spotted the riverboat getting close.

"There it is, the riverboat. It won't be long now."

The three men waited until the boat slowly docked before they approached. The captain seeing them waved and lowered the bridge for them to board again.

"Wasn't expecting to see yous three again so soon. Yous changed your minds about going south?"

"Nope, only wanted to ask you a few questions that we didn't want to ask whilst that Ranger was near."

"Oh. Well, I can wait a few minutes, what are the questions? I'm happy to help or answer them if'n I can. And no need for any formalities, I know yous is all Private Investigators, the old fellar told me that."

"Can you tell us if an Apache has recently stepped onto the deck of this stern-wheeler?" Tyrell asked as cordially as he could.

"An Apache? Nope, can't say I've seen any Apache, let me guess yous is looking for the Apache Kid, rumored to be in these parts?"

"Rumored?" Tyrell questioned with uncertainty.

"I reckon so. I heard it was all horseshit. The Apache Kid has been dead for a few years from what I understand. Got himself shot up or something, by some cattle rancher that is what I've been lead to understand."

"As far as we know, there ain't no truth to that, we've been tracking him for a few weeks already, and he has indeed been sighted. You might be thinking the Apache Kid might dress like an Apache, long hair and such, but that is far from the truth. He dresses no different than either of us standing here, he might wear moccasins and he'd be packing a .50 caliber Hawken. You couldn't miss that, nor the horse he might have been riding, a white one."

"Well, you're right about what I might have thought the Kid to look like. You hear a word like Apache and you're mind conjures up an Apache warrior," the captain chuckled.

"There was a fella a few days back was darker colored skin, short black hair wearing a low brow hat, and rode an Appaloosa. He didn't say two words about nothing, and was the only passenger that crossed on that trip, he did indeed have a Hawken. Shit, you saying that was the Apache Kid?"

"Chances are. So, a fella did cross here packing a .50 caliber Hawken and was riding an Appaloosa?" Tyrell wanted to be clear.

"Yes indeed. By the time I had this boat turned around, he was gone. I ain't sure which way he went after that, other than he stepped off right here. I hope I've helped yous with some answers, but, I got to get back to the other side, got a schedule I'm required to follow."

"You were a great help, thank you. One other question does the outpost up river from here have a general store?"

"It does, has a telegraph office too and a small saloon. Fort Shepherd don't have a saloon, nor a public telegraph office, only a mercantile and a Mounted Police station, with two redcoats usually on duty."

"All right, I guess we'll let you get back on schedule, thanks again for your help in answering a few questions we had," Tyrell said as the three of them once more stepped onto the loading bridge, and made their way back to where they had watched the riverboat leave before.

"Well, I guess we know now that someone, maybe the Apache Kid did cross here, and that the outpost up river has a telegraph office, saloon, and general store. It is about ten miles up. Think we ought to head that way, we could spend the night there, and pick up supplies in the morning, send off a wire to Ed and head back this way and onward to Fort Shepherd."

"That'd add a few more miles onto our trek to Fort Shepherd, but, it ain't got no saloon or telegraph office. Probably would be best to go up river, like you say Travis we could send off a wire leastwise back to McCoy's, let them know where we are, why we're here and what it is we've learned," Riley pointed out.

"I'd agree, besides a shot of whisky or two does sound good."

"All right, let's get. We got ten miles to go and daylight is burning up," Tyrell said as the three of them headed westerly along the Columbia River trail.

"Did it say on that map of yours the name of the place up yon?" Riley questioned as they sauntered on.

Tyrell reached into his saddlebags and pulled the map out, slowing their horses to a stop they gathered around.

"There is the Columbia River outpost on that side and up here a few, there it is. Beacon Hill outpost, there must be a lighthouse or beacon around the area."

"Or it is jus' named that for no particular reason."

"Or that, yep," Tyrell replied.

"Off to Beacon Hill we go."

Heeling their horses flanks they continued on, Black Dog tailing close behind.

Chapter 13

The Beacon Hill outpost finally came into view a couple hours later. It was certainly livelier than the Columbia River outpost that the three of them had left behind that day. There were even a couple of people on the wooden boardwalk in front of the saloon.

They nodded at the two men as they dismounted and tethered their horses. The two men nodded back.

"Can you point us in the direction of the telegraph office?" Tyrell asked as they stepped up onto the boardwalk.

The one man pointed down the street to an old building made from log.

"Jack ain't there though. He ain't due back until later."

"Jack is the telegrapher I take it?"

"He's only one knows how to tap, tap, tap, out the words," the man smiled.

"All right, thank you mister," Tyrell nodded his appreciation and the three of them stepped into the town saloon and found a table to sit at. Looking around they were expecting to see Lee Griffith, but he was nowhere in sight.

"Wonder where our friend Lee got too?" Riley questioned. "I don't see him, would have thought he'd be here."

"Could've carried onward I suppose, or he turned south," Tyrell said as the barmaid made her way over to them. She was dressed in denim from top to bottom and around her waist, she was packing a pearl handled .45, and she looked like she could use it too.

"Afternoon, gentlemen, what can I get for you?"

"A round of whisky and a jug of draft, please," Tyrell said as he looked up to her.

"Anything else?" she questioned.

"That'll do for now, I do have a question though?"

"Oh, what might that be?"

"Was there a man here a while ago, he was a Yank?"

"There sure was, he left after he spoke with Clyde, and in a quick hurry too I might add."

"Clyde? Who might that be?"

"Clyde is the town law enforcer, he ain't a lawman though, and really doesn't have any formal training, but, he keeps the town folk safe."

"He's a gunman?" Colby questioned.

"He sure is, can draw a pistol quicker than any man in these parts, most hoodwinks that come through here to take the riverboat on their way to God knows where, don't mess with Clyde. Those that do, end up getting buried," she smiled at the three of them.

"Is there any chance we could meet him, we work for McCoy's out of Fort Macleod, this here is Riley and Colby, and I'm Travis."

"McCoy's?" she questioned, "and what is McCoy's?"

"Sorry about that ma'am, McCoy's Private Investigations and Security."

"Uh-huh, and what brings the three of you this way? Fort Macleod is quite the distance away."

Tyrell nodded, "it sure is ma'am, we've been tracking a fugitive and it just so happens that it might be, that Yank that was here is also looking for the same man," he wasn't sure of that but for now it was a tale that would suffice.

The saloon door swung open and in stepped one of the men that they had seen on the boardwalk.

"Well, look at that. There is Clyde now. I'll send him over," she said as she pranced away and had a few words with Clyde, who looked over to where the three of them were seated. Clyde nodded to her and made his way over to the table.

"Marsha tells me, the three of you wanted to have words with me, that you're Private Investigators or something from down east. What can I help yous with?" Clyde asked as he pulled up a chair and sat down.

"That's right, I'm Travis, this is Colby and Riley we work for McCoy's Private Investigations and Security. Marsha tells us that you spoke with a Yank earlier today."

"Yeah, and what of it?"

"I guess he took off in a quick hurry after he spoke with you."

"He did, needed to catch the next riverboat up river some."

"You don't mind if I asked what you two talked about?" Tyrell questioned as Marsha brought them their draft and whisky and an extra glass for Clyde.

"Nope not at all. He asked when the next riverboat on this side headed up river. I told him and he left."

"He didn't ask you anything else?" Riley questioned as he poured each of them a draft, and shot back his whisky.

Clyde took a swallow from his draft, and looked at Riley.

"Said he was trailing a fugitive, nothing more and nothing less, I knew right off the start he was a Yank lawman, and now you three are here. I reckon yous is looking for a fugitive too."

Clyde finished the last swallow of his draft.

"So, my turn to ask a question now, who is it a Yank and three prairie chickens might be looking for?"

"Prairie chickens?" Colby questioned as though it were an insult.

"Look I didn't mean anything by it, that is what we call prairie folk around here."

"I don't think I like that much, sounds like an insult to me," Colby added as he leaned back in his chair.

Clyde chuckled.

"Like I said it don't mean a thing."

Although it seemed things were getting heated up, they really weren't. Riley poured Clyde another draft.

"Thank you, 'Riley', it was right?"

Riley nodded 'yes' as he took a swallow from his own draft.

"To answer your earlier question Clyde, the three of us are indeed looking for a fugitive, been tracking him since late December, he's known by a couple of different names, his real name though is Ski-be-nan-ted," Riley finished.

Clyde looked at the three of them in amusement and chuckled.

"Shit, I'd know that name anywhere, you three are looking for a damn ghost, the Apache Kid is dead. Been dead for years from what I know. Was shot I heard by a rancher down south."

"Them are the tales that are told around fires, he ain't dead though Clyde, he's been spotted a few different times and the three of us have been tracking him," Tyrell made clear.

The news of the Apache Kid's appearance in and around Alberta and British Columbia had not obviously made it to the Beacon Hill outpost, and if it had no one believed it.

"So, you're saying that Ski-be-nan-ted is in and around these parts?" Clyde wanted to be sure he was hearing, what it was he was hearing.

"Yep, he also crossed the Columbia River, was a passenger according the riverboat captain a few days back, maybe a week."

Clyde looked over to Colby who had spoken.

"That riverboat captain tells a lot of bullshit, he once told me that he had seen and talked with Billy the Kid nine or ten years after his death. Nope, I wouldn't believe much of what he says."

"That might be farfetched, but, we've been tracking the Apache Kid for a while I can tell you that. Whether or not the captain told you a story about Billy or not don't mean he ain't saw Ski-be-nan-ted. I believe what he said to be true, since we tracked him to the Columbia River outpost."

"If it is true, I can tell yous that no one I've seen over the last while that has passed through here looked anything like the Apache Kid."

"You see everybody that comes through here, Clyde?" Colby asked with a mild sneer.

"I never said that. If anyone with the reputation like that of the Apache Kid passed through here, someone would have seen him."

"That is right, someone did, the riverboat captain."

Clyde shook his head, "or that is what he claims."

Finally, Tyrell jumped into the conversation.

"Look, we ain't here to debate the honesty of the riverboat captain, or your obvious hate for the man, but, I can assure you Clyde, that we've been tracking Ski-be-nan-ted, and his trail pretty much lead us to this side of the Columbia River. Whether or not he came this way is anyone's guess. Did you happen to see a man come through here riding an Appaloosa anytime recently?"

"There was one fella, but he didn't stop here, rode right on by. But, he weren't the Kid, I can tell you that."

"How can you be sure, if he didn't stop?"

"It was a branded horse, I saw the brand."

"That don't mean a thing, maybe he stole the horse."

Clyde looked at his glass of draft.

"I guess that could be. Never quite considered that, I can tell you the brand was that of the Elquin Ranch, sixty miles west and the direction that man and Appaloosa were traveling. The brand tells me he was heading home.

Maybe you three should go there ask if they've had any horses stolen," Clyde responded with little care.

"The Elquin Ranch you say?"

"That is what I said. The Elquin Ranch, a few miles northwest of the town of Crab Apple, their brand is an E-q- and an R, and that Appaloosa was branded as such."

Clyde took the last swig of his draft and stood up.

"I have other things to tend to, so, I wish yous luck in finding a ghost," he said as he tilted his hat and walked away.

"Jesus Christ, a sixty-mile ride west to find out if the Elquin Ranch has had any horses stolen, seems like a long way to go to find out one way or the other."

"That it is Colby, a damn hindrance is what it is, but, we're gathering leads and it is all part of the job at hand. Besides, it is the direction who we think to be the Apache Kid was heading," Riley said as he waved the barmaid, Marsha, back over to order another round of whisky.

"Damn, he said Crab Apple didn't he?"

Tyrell's mind drifted to his encounter with Serena Boalee a year or so earlier in the same town, while he was surprisingly enough tracking down Matt Crawford for the first time. The more he thought of her now, the more Marsha, the barmaid reminded him of her. He looked at her as she brought them their next round of whisky it was almost uncanny. They dressed alike, wore pistols around their waists and were obviously not afraid to use them. The deep look on Tyrell's face caught Riley's attention as he shot back his whisky.

"What is it Travis, looks like you're drifting."

Tyrell blinked and shook his head.

"I was. I've been through Crab Apple, when I went looking for Matt that first time, and then later found and brought in Atalmore, and Colby," he chuckled at how odd it seemed, as he looked over to Colby, who was now also reminiscing about that time, thanks to Tyrell's mentioning of it.

He looked at Tyrell and shook his head, as the memory of Tyrell convincing Atalmore, the others, and himself to throw down their arms because they were surrounded by ten men, when in all actuality it had only been two. It had changed his life though, and he was grateful for that.

"Was jus' thinking about a woman I met there, is all. Marsha reminded me of her," Tyrell brought his shot of whisky to his lips and tilted his head back as he downed it.

"A woman?" Riley was smirking.

"Indeed she was, Riley. Serena Boalee. Her folks own the stable up that way. Crab Apple ain't much of a town, from what I recall. It is a damn long ride from here though, that is for sure, and to be honest, I ain't looking forward to the travel, don't mind one bit though looking in on Serena if we do decide to go there."

"There ain't nothing to be decided. Clyde has pointed us to a possible lead, the direction he saw the rider and Appaloosa traveling. It is our lawful duty to follow that Appaloosa and the lead, if we don't come upon something between here and there, that decides for us otherwise," Riley said as he spun his shot glass like a spinning-top on the table.

"I suppose there ain't no arguing that fact. Let's finish these drafts and get. The sooner we hit the trail the sooner we'll find out, what, if anything comes from it. As you say Riley, that Appaloosa and rider headed west anyway, could be we might learn more as we travel."

"I can't figure out any reason the Kid would go west, seems like a long route to go to Big Muddy, he'd have to turn east and cross the Rocky Mountains, and that don't make a lick of sense to me."

"Maybe he ain't heading to Big Muddy, Colby. Perhaps like what Crying Wolf said when we left him, there are those in these parts that would give him sanctuary. Could be he's heading into Blackfoot territory, or maybe even the Ksanka territory."

"What about that froze body we found, we ain't reported that yet, and the closest Mounted Police station is Fort Shepherd. Which ain't west, it is south."

"We'll send a wire off to Ed in that regard, Colby, before we leave here. He'll inform the law in due course. It don't make much sense to travel all that way back down river to report that, when we have new information that might pertain to the Apache Kid going west."

With nothing more being added, or said, the three of them stood up and exited the small saloon. Making their way over to the telegraph office, Tyrell wrote out what needed to be sent to Ed, his only hope was the telegrapher got the message correct, the smell of whisky on his breath was overwhelming, and told the story that he was obviously half drunk.

Finally, sending the wire off to McCoy's they swung back up on their rides and headed west along the Columbia River in the direction of Crab Apple, and the direction that Lee Griffith travelled as well as whom they knew to be Ski-be-nan-ted *aka* the Apache Kid.
Ed and Brady were about to close up shop for the day when Buz brought them the telegram.

"Glad I caught you, Ed, before you closed up. I got another telegram for you. It is as confusing as hell, but, I did my best in transcribing it."

He handed the telegram over to Ed, who looked it over and frowned.

"I'd say it is damn confusing," he handed it to Brady. "What do you make of that?" he questioned.

Brady looked it over and read it.

"From what I can make of it is that Travis and the others is heading west to Crab Apple, they got a lead on the Kid I'd assume. There is also something in here about a man froze near some bridge. It reads like this; 'In be a con hill, Skin bad tan, heading west, Crab Apples, found dead a man froze near creek'. I think 'be a con hill' is Beacon Hill, and 'Skin bad tan' is supposed to be 'Ski-be-nan-ted', that is the only thing that makes sense. The frozen man thing near a creek, well that don't make much sense. The telegrapher must've been drunk," Brady coincided as he looked it over again, and shook his head.

He handed it back to Ed, who looked again and agreed that is how it was likely supposed to read.

"Thanks for bringing this to us Buz, I think we got it figured out."

"I'm sure glad you were able to make sense of it, 'cause I certainly couldn't, I'd agree with Brady, the telegrapher must've been drunk," Buz chuckled and shook his head as he turned and exited.

"You really think that is what was supposed to be in this telegram, Brady?"

"It is the only thing that makes sense isn't it. Beacon Hill is an outpost along the Columbia River's west side, they were likely heading to Fort Shepherd, and picked up the Kid's trail."

Brady made his way over to the map on the wall and looked at it.

"There is a creek they would have needed to cross, could be that is the creek that is mentioned regarding the frozen man."

Brady shrugged, "I don't know, old man. I do think the rest of what we assume is how it is."

"So, they're heading west to Crab Apple, and possibly found a man frozen in a creek. Shit, that ain't much to go on."

"No it ain't but it is something, least we know they're alive and well, and that is all that matters. We'll have to wait and see what comes of it, and hope they send us another telegram in the coming days."

Ed nodded in agreement as they continued to lock up for the day.

"I was hoping that at least Travis and Riley would be back before my gracious retirement, I don't think that'll be the case now though."

"Ah, we'll celebrate your retirement when they make it back. Besides I ain't truly convinced you will retire old man."

"I have every intention to retire, Brady. I made that promise to myself and I plan on keeping it," Ed responded as they made their way to the horse corral and saddled up.

"I'll believe it when I see it old man, 'til then, well, as I said, I ain't convinced."

The two rode off in the direction of home, as the evening sun fell behind the western horizon. Another workday at McCoy's had ended.

Chapter 14

Tyrell, Riley, and Colby had travelled for two hours and now had to make a choice. They could wait for the riverboat to return from up river or they could follow the southwest trail, which, ultimately, would lead them to the same place that the boat would dock.

"Here is where we need to decide if we should wait for the boat, or continue onward along the trail, if we stay here we have a couple of small shelters and fire pits we could use to keep the chill away."

"How much longer do you figure we'd have to wait for that boat?" Colby questioned.

"Hard to say, I'd hope it'd show up soon. Might not see it though until morning," Tyrell responded as he looked west.

"Morning? Shit, I hope not. We could carry on along the trail in that case and likely be closer to our destination than we are now," Riley added.

"I know you don't like riverboats, Riley, but it knocks off about fifteen or twenty miles of travel time. If the Kid went this way as we suspect, he would've travelled up river on that boat. It would put him back on the right side of the Columbia, in less time. I think traveling the trail would have slowed him down, and in the end if we decide to carry on, it will slow us down too. I think we're better off staying put, there is shelter here leastwise."

"Since there ain't no tell tale sign of which way he went, I figure we should wait for the boat too, 'specially if it saves us twenty miles of trail riding," Colby suggested.

"All right, well, since the two of you figure waiting for the boat is best, then, we should get a fire going in one of these fire pits and brew some coffee, while we wait," Riley said as he tethered his horse, and found some wood to get a fire lit.

It didn't take long to get settled, and now huddled under one of the small shelters with a fire burning and coffee brewing, things weren't so bad, and the waiting became more of a well deserved rest.

Finally, in the distance they could hear the boat as it approached. It wasn't quite dark yet when it docked, but it was certainly going to make for an interesting journey up river.

Two passengers stepped off and nodded to the three of them as they boarded. The captain was a burly man in his late fifties. He greeted them with a gritty smile as they made their way onto the deck and tethered their horses.

"You three and that dog are lucky to be here, this is the last trip up river today. She is going to be a rough one too, had some whitecaps tossing and turning us as we made our way down. Going back up we'll likely see the same. So, keep your hats on."

The captain chuckled as he backed away from the boat landing and closed the off ramp bridge. With a few deep turns, the boat was finally facing up river.

"There we go, all set now. The trip up river should take about an hour give or take, depending of course on what the Columbia throws at us. There are ropes in the deck boxes should we need them," the captain pointed at a few big wooden boxes that lined the side of the deck.

Riley looked over to Tyrell and shook his head.

"Did you hear that Travis, ropes. I don't know why I let you folks always talk me into trains and boats, goddamn it, I must be a sucker waiting on a heart attack."

"Think of it this way, Riley, the boat will take us an hour to get up river, the trail would take a half days ride, maybe longer, depending on what the trail threw at us…" Tyrell smirked at his paraphrase.

Colby chuckled.

"It won't be all that bad Riley, Travis don't know how to swim, so if you do, make sure to toss him a rope when we go under."

Riley's eyes grew big and he shook his head.

"Go under! Jesus Christ, Colby, quit making jokes. I don't know how to swim either."

"Shit, let's hope there are enough ropes," Colby teased.

For thirty minutes, Riley bickered and complained. Finally, he relented and calmed down enough to enjoy the sometime rough, but always beautiful journey up the Columbia. Now as he looked around at what he could see of the sky, and distant shores, he relaxed.

He stood next to both Travis, Colby, and Black Dog near the bow and watched with them as the sun slowly dissipated leaving behind the brilliant colors of a spectacular sunset.

"That right there makes all the doubt I had about riverboats unjustifiable. That is something, ain't it?" he questioned as they stood there and looked on.

"It sure is. Damn spectacular is what that is."

The captain was now standing beside them taking in the same view and it startled Riley for a brief moment, but nothing else seemed to matter but the view.

"That is one of the benefits being a riverboat captain. I get to see stuff like that. That one though, tonight is one of the better ones I've seen lately. It means for a cold evening and a warm day. 'A red sky and night is a sailor's delight', or so they say."

The four men and Black Dog stood in silence for a few brief minutes, finally, the captain turned heel and headed back to the stern and took over the helm once again. The shore and boat landing came into view a short while later and he slowly pulled the vessel in and docked.

"Land ho!" he hollered with a smile. "Once I get the bridge down, you can un-tether your horses. It keeps them from getting riled at the sound, hang on."

It took a minute or so, but finally he gave them the signal to go ahead and off load. Before they did, they spoke with him and asked a few questions once they introduced who they were.

Before we go, Captain, you don't mind if we ask you a few questions do you."

"Depends on what you ask, I reckon."

"The three of us work for McCoy's Private Investigations and Security, out of Fort Macleod. I'm Travis this is Riley, and Colby. We've been tracking a man that rides an Appaloosa and packs a .50 caliber Hawken, the captain down river at the Columbia River outpost claims to have seen him, on his boat a few days ago. Is there any chance you've seen the same man on your vessel?"

"Oh yeah, they boarded all right, the man didn't speak much, kept his head tilted forward for the better part of the trip, he boarded four or five days ago on the last trip up river as well, was the only passenger on that trip. He was certainly riding an Appaloosa, and there was indeed a Hawken strapped to his saddle. What is he wanted for, or is he?"

"He is wanted all right, if we are correct on our assumptions that man was Ski-be-nan-ted, also known as the Apache Kid."

The captain's jaw dropped and his eyes grew big with surprise and shock.

"Holy shit! I had the Apache Kid on my vessel, well now don't that beat all," he said with glee. He was certainly excited about the fact. "I can't believe that, Jesus, that is something…huh. I heard he had been killed a long time ago."

"That seems to be what most have heard and what most seem to believe, but, he is alive as he has ever been. You didn't happen to see which direction he went once he off loaded did you?" Tyrell asked.

"Sure did, he headed northwesterly. There are a few different trails that head in all four directions up yon some, so I ain't got a clue where he might have went after that, but, I saw him head northerly."

Tyrell nodded his appreciation.

"Uh-huh, well, thank you Captain for the information, there ain't nothing else we need to know," Tyrell said as the three of them turned their horses and walked off the ramp onto solid ground. They carried on northwesterly for a spell, Black Dog trailing close behind. When it became too dark to ride, they found a suitable place to settle in for the evening.

"Right here I reckon will do," Tyrell said as they pulled their horses up to the small clearing on the side of the trail. The snow wasn't too deep there and by the time they had their camp set up it had all been packed down and stirred up. Finding enough wood to get them through the night, they lit a fire, brewed coffee, and Riley went ahead and threw together beans and biscuits.

"Either of you been taking notes on what it is we've learned so far about the Kid, and riverboat crossings?" Tyrell asked as he slurped from his tin cup of coffee. He had learned something and wanted to see if they had figured it out too.

"Seems to me he's running us around in circles, he crossed down river to get to the other side, then crossed back to this side, also seems to keep his head tilted, I reckon so his face can't be distinguished," Colby volunteered his answer.

"What about you Riley, is there anything you're picking up on?"

"Yeah, he likes riverboats, to be honest Travis, I think I'd go with Colby's answer."

"Well, you're both right then, but, also, he seems to be the only passenger and he's boarding them on the last trip of the day. That to me spells out that he must have been watching the boats come and go, and boards when there are no other passengers. That is what I've learned."

"Huh, damn, that is a good observation," Riley said as he looked into the flames of their evening fire, and contemplated Tyrell's observation.

"Too bad there ain't any other riverboat landings, between here and Crab Apple, though," Tyrell pointed out.

"We isn't sure he carried on that way yet though are we?"

"Nope, we are not, Colby. But, if we pick up his trail and it leads to another river crossing along the way, we can be sure he waited for the last trip of the day, and only boarded if there weren't any other passengers."

"Well, I ain't sure what that does for us? He is ahead of us by almost a week Travis."

"That is the downside of the observation, I suppose," Tyrell took a swallow from his coffee.

"It does tell us a little bit about him though; he knows he is being looked for, and is taking precautions to not be seen," Riley responded.

"Of course he would, Riley. He's on the run and he's doing a fine job at running too. Has kept ahead of us even when we was close to him, he vanished…maybe we are looking for a ghost."

"He'll make a mistake, Colby, folks on the run always do, I don't reckon the Kid is any different. We keep on him, and we'll find him," Riley was certain of that. He had been in the business for a long time and he knew that even the most adept at evading the law, were, eventually caught.

Evening came and evening went, and at the first sign of daylight on the 8th of January the three of them once more saddled up and continued on their way, not certain which way they were going to end up going by day's end. They continued westerly, heading toward Crab Apple.

"You figure what that fella back at the Beacon Hill outpost said about that Appaloosa and rider, is true, Travis, that it belonged to the Elquin Ranch?" Colby asked.

"I don't reckon Clyde had any reason to lie. It is our best lead so far, and when we finally make it there, I guess we'll know one way or the other."

"'Less of course, we get side tracked again, can never know what lies ahead, and we've only be riding for about an hour. A sixty mile ride might see us in Crab Apple in a couple days, between now and then, anything can happen."

"You got that right, Riley," Tyrell responded as they sped up their horses to a slow canter and continued in silence.

Coming to a cross roads now, they slowed their horses down and stopped. Tyrell pulled out his dilapidated old map and he looked it over. Bringing his hand to his chin he contemplated, then nodded.

"This is where the trail turns easterly, according to this map up ahead about twenty or so miles, it turns northerly. Right over the Rocky Mountains. I don't see no other roads or trails going south like the Captain mentioned."

"That seems odd to you, Travis, even though that map in your hand is about as old as Colby."

"It ain't turned us wrong yet, Riley."

"It don't matter none, I didn't want to say anything earlier on, but…ah, where is the closest town?" Riley asked.

It was the tone of his voice as he said that, that made Tyrell, look at him.

"What is going on, Riley, you is split open ain't ya, from that bullet wound?"

Tyrell swung off his horse, made his way over to Riley and looked at him.

"C'mon, Riley, pull up that goddamn shirt of yours, or I'll rip you off that horse and do it myself, you crazy son-of-a-bitch! I told you if you start bleeding out or have any pain, you were supposed to tell me," Tyrell though, could already see the blood soaking through Riley's shirt.

"Hang on, Jesus, Travis, I don't need no mothering."

"Mothering my ass! This is about the job at hand. You can't be riding these trails with a goddamn bullet wound, and one that is bleeding. You are jeopardizing the operation. Now get down off that horse, I need to see what the hell."

Tyrell was livid, yet at the same time quite concerned about Riley's well being, especially since they were miles away from any town that might have a doctor.

Riley slid off his horse with Colby and Tyrell's help. They sat him down on a log and he pulled up his shirt. Sure enough, blood was trickling down his side. Realizing then that the tourniquet wasn't doing the job anymore, Tyrell shook his head.

"When did you start noticing that you're bleeding, Riley?"

"Not too long ago. I'll be all right though, jus' need to have a rest, maybe tighten up the bandage some, and we can get moving again."

"That tourniquet ain't doing nothing for you Riley. Tightening it ain't going to make a bit of difference. You need a damn doctor, and some catgut to mend it some. We should have had that looked at back at Beacon Hill."

"I reckon she started to bleed due to the galloping and whatnot that we've been doing today. It has only been since, that she split open," Riley pointed out as he tucked his shirt back in.

"No matter, you keep bleeding as you are, and you'll need a couple pints of whisky to fill up them old veins of yours. Nope, we have to turn back Riley, you need a doctor."

"Jesus Christ, what are you saying, Travis. That we have to head back the way we came, and start this damn ride again in a couple more days?"

"That is exactly what I'm saying, Colby. We might only see a trickling of blood, but, under that garment we got wrapped around him is probably a bloody mess and he's probably bleeding a lot worse than what we're seeing. The dam has broke."

"I don't want to head back, Travis. I'd rather we continued on, there has to be a homestead or small town around here somewhere. It jus' ain't on that old map of yours."

"No way, Riley, we can't risk that. You could die before we find any help, we know help may be sought a few hours ride back the way we came. Could make the riverboat back to Beacon Hill in four or five hours, I'd rather do that than possibly watch you die."

"If I'm possibly dying, Travis, grant this dying man one last wish," Riley said as he looked at him sternly, "tighten up this goddamn tourniquet, hand me my whisky bottle and let's get on with it and continue west. No need to go back."

"That right there is more than one wish, Riley."

"What if, help going westerly is two hours or less away, whereas we know help going back is near five or six? You see where I'm going with that, Travis."

"Goddamn it Riley, I don't know. Could be there ain't no help west of here until Crab Apple, and that there is two days ride."

"I got some fishing line in my saddlebag, Travis. You could use that to sew me up, you can gather that whilst you get me my whisky."

"I don't like what you're asking one damn bit, Riley."

"You know it as well as me Travis that it would work, for now at least."

Colby was already rummaging through Riley's saddlebags for the items.

"He's right, we can sew him up with the line and clean it up with his whisky," Colby said as he finally found what he was looking for.

"No, no, I want the whisky to drink, whilst you sew me up."

"Whatever is left after we clean it up, you can drink, you ain't getting a damn slurp until then."

"Well, Jesus, that don't seem fair, Colby."

"It don't matter none, if you hadn't got yourself shot in the first place, you could drink it all for all I care."

Tyrell who was standing nearby and listening couldn't believe what it was that he was being talked into.

"You seriously, want me to sew you up with fishing line?"

"Damn right I do. Turning back, will slow us down and I want to get on with it, so we can head back to Fort Macleod, and my own damn bed," Riley said with weariness. "Would like to get there before spring," he added as a joke.

"Shit. All right Riley, we'll do it your way, you die on this trail though, and I'll shoot you myself. We got to get a fire started first, c'mon Colby lets gather some wood."

A short while later after a fire had been started, Tyrell had Riley pull up his shirt, he removed the blood soaked tourniquet, and Colby doused the wound with whisky. Riley inhaled deeply and squinted as Tyrell now wiped away at the wound with the cleaner part of the tourniquet.

"Stings a bit does it, Riley?"

"Damn right," he said as he reached for the bottle of whisky in Colby's hand. Colby' though didn't let him have it.

"We ain't done, yet Riley."

"Goddamn it Colby, I just want a swallow."

"Nope, not 'til we know that she's cleaned up enough to sew your hide."

"All right, splash some more on there, Colby," Tyrell said as he swabbed the wound again. He could see the wound now that it was cleaned up. He folded up the tourniquet and had Riley hold it in place while he threaded the line through the fishing hook.

"This is probably going to hurt a bit, you might want to piss now so you don't when I stick the hook and line in ya," Tyrell teased as he pulled the line through the hook eye. The line now tied off, he leaned forward.

"Okay, Riley, move your hand, Colby give him his whisky," he said as he stuck the hook through Riley's flesh. Riley took a long swallow from the whisky bottle, and nodded to him to proceed as he took another swig. Now with the wound stitched in three places, Colby once more doused the wound with whisky, then handed the bottle back to a half drunk Riley.

Tyrell swabbed the wound one last time.

"I reckon that is the best I can do, she ain't bleeding now. I'll wrap it up with the other piece of my long-johns."

"You do whatever it is you need to do, Travis I'm fine," Riley said as he looked into the flames of their fire. "I told ya's it'd work didn't I? I feel better already," he said as he took another gulp from the whisky bottle in his hand.

Both Tyrell and Colby knew it was the whisky talking. He might feel fine now, but he would certainly feel it when the whisky wore off.

"Can you ride, Riley?"

"I think so. You want to start off again?" Riley questioned in a slur.

"Not just yet, nope. I think we'll get some coffee going since we already have a fire. We'll rest a while first. Got plenty of daylight left," Tyrell said as he added snow to the pot, and set it close to the fire to melt down, then adding grinds he set it in the flames. It didn't take long and he poured Riley a cup, and took back what was left of the whisky.

"Drink this up Riley," he handed the coffee over to him. "You still feeling all right?"

"Am so," Riley said as he began to stand with coffee in hand to only sit back down. "Okay, maybe I need to sit for a bit," he chuckled.

"We'll get a couple of coffees into you first, I reckon. Can't be riding drunk."

"Drunk? Shit, I'm only gingerly drunk, I ain't drunk."

"A drunk always denies his drunkenness, you are drunk Riley, you drank near half a bottle straight up," Colby said as he took a swallow of coffee.

Chapter 15

An hour or so later, after finishing the pot of coffee, Riley was sober enough to ride, and the three of them along with Black Dog carried on west.

"How are you holding up there, Riley?" Tyrell asked after they had been riding for a while.

"I'm doing fine. The stitches sting a bit, but I'm okay. You did a good job I reckon in sewn me up."

"You ain't bleeding none?'

"Not as far as I can tell, nope."

"All right, maybe you will live."

"You said that like you weren't expecting me too," Riley chuckled as they carried on.

Sometime later, they could smell smoke and in the distance, Colby could see smoke rising.

"Looks like up ahead, there might be a homestead," he pointed to the sky.

"Looks that way, don't it."

"We going to stop when we get there, Travis?"

"What the hell do we need to stop for, Colby?" Riley interjected.

"Maybe get that wound looked at again, make any adjustments."

"Nah, I don't need no more adjusting. We could stop though, and ask if they may have seen an Appaloosa and rider come this way, the more leads we can get the better, I reckon. Don't need no one looking me over, I'm fine."

"I guess it all depends if the smoke rising comes from a homestead and how far off the trail it might be. If it is near, stopping probably ain't such a bad idea. Let's hope they're the friendly sort," Tyrell now replied as they traipsed onward.

Twenty minutes later the trail opened up to flat land of sort, and in the distance they could make out cattle roaming the fenced off fields, and past the field a house stood smoke billowing from its chimney. They slowed their horses to a halt and looked on.

"It looks like a cattle ranch, not too far away, figure we should swing up there?"

"Couldn't hurt none, I don't reckon. Like Riley says, maybe we can get another lead on the Kid."

All in agreement, they turned their steeds and headed up along the road that led to the ranch. The house looked odd as big as it was and out in the middle of nowhere. As they approached a couple of ranch hands, on horses met them before they made the distance.

"This here is private land misters. What is your purpose of being here?" one of the riders asked as they halted their horses and waited for a response.

"My name is Travis, this is Colby and Riley, we're Private Investigators and Security Personnel, from Fort Macleod, we work for McCoy's," Tyrell pulled out his credentials and showed them to the man who spoke.

"That is what that says all right, still didn't answer my question though."

"I ain't got to that yet. We've been trailing a man on an Appaloosa, he may have come this way, by chance have yous seen anyone like that?"

"Appaloosa… nope can't say as we have. Ain't saw any rider in the last while 'cept you three and the dog."

"Is it possible someone else may have seen a man on an Appaloosa?"

The man shrugged.

"Don't know. I know I ain't saw anyone like that."

He looked over to the rider beside him.

"What about you, Reg, you ever see an Appaloosa and rider come by here lately?"

Reg, simply shook his head 'no'.

"There you have it misters, we ain't saw no man on an Appaloosa, the Elquin Ranch a day or so ride west has a bunch of Appaloosa's, they're the only ones 'round here that have that breed."

"We know about the Elquin Ranch and we're heading that way, now."

"Anyone with an Appaloosa would've likely come from there, is one of their men wanted for something?"

"I don't reckon. The rider we're talking about though is, and he was riding an Appaloosa with a big old .50 caliber Hawken strapped to the horses scabbard."

"Nope, ain't saw anyone packing a Hawken either."

"All right, well, thank you for your time. We'll get."

"Hold up, it is getting late and you three seem like you're legit, if'n yous like we can offer you a hot meal and a place to sleep for the night."

"That is kind of you," Tyrell looked over to Colby and Riley. "You two want a hot meal and place to sleep tonight?"

"Damn right."

"All right. We'll take you up on that offer, we wouldn't be intruding would we?"

"Not at all. I'm Jack and this is Reg, we work for the Hurley's whose ranch house you see up ahead."

"Well, nice to meet you, Jack, Reg, and thank you kindly once again for your offer."

"Miss Hurley, wouldn't have it any other way since you are decent men, and if we sent you off without a hot meal and place to sleep at this time of day, she'd tear us both new ones. C'mon let's get," Jack said as he and Reg turned their steeds and the others followed.

"How big is Hurley ranch?" Colby asked to make conversation as they continue.

"It employees a dozen men and has over eight hundred head of cattle," Jack answered back.

"That is a big operation. Most of the cattle go to auction then?"

"Correct, we run them east in spring and fall, right into Calgary. Most time we come back with a few head too."

"Ever have any issues with cattle rustlers?"

"With a dozen well armed men and twenty-four hour shifts, never had a problem for as long as I've been here, and I've been here ten years. The cattle is all branded and ear tagged. We run white-faced cattle most of the time, but, we've had black-angus too."

By now, they were pulling up to the house, and met once more by another four men.

"What you got there, Jack?"

"Some riders from Fort Macleod, been trailing a man on an Appaloosa. They is lawmen of sort, Private Investigators, I've seen their credentials," Jack responded as he swung off his horse.

"You must work for McCoy's, yes?" The man standing on the porch asked as Tyrell, Riley and Colby tethered their horses.

"That we do, you have heard of them?"

"I hired Ed McCoy a few years back, he only had his son working with him then."

"That'd be Brady McCoy."

"That is right. He and Brady did some work for me down south. I'm Chester Hurley, and you folks are?"

"I'm Travis, this is Colby and Riley," Tyrell responded as he introduced them.

"Well, Travis, Riley, and Colby, welcome to Hurly ranch. That dog of yours, don't chase cattle, does he?"

"No sir. He'd guard them more than anything else, his name is Black Dog, and he won't worry your cattle none."

"All right, well, I'll have mother build you some food, come in," he gestured for them to follow him, while the others who had been standing beside him made their way back to the bunkhouse and work at hand, Black Dog simply laid down on the stoop, he wasn't going anywhere.

The three of them followed Chester into the big house. Mounted on the walls above the fireplace hearth in the living area were mounts of mule deer, antelope, a black bear, and mountain lion. The living area was scattered with red velvet high-back Victorian furniture. It was ritzy.

"Nice place you have here Mr. Hurley," Colby pointed out as he looked around. "You is a hunter too I see."

"Every now and again, I do hunt, but not as much as I'd like. There is nothing like being out in the woods with a couple good friends, shooting the shit sitting around a fire and hunting things to eat." Chester chuckled. He gestured for them to take a seat. "Make yourselves comfortable, I'll go let mother know to put a hot meal together, likely just be what we had for dinner tonight." Chester turned and walked into another room leaving the three of them sitting.

"This place is huge," Riley said as he looked around.

"It sure is, bigger than life itself ain't it?"

Tyrell stood up, walked over to the fireplace hearth, and looked on the wall at the animals mounted there. A few minutes later Chester returned.

"Mother said she'll have some vittles for yous shortly. Roast beef and fixings. I see you have taken a liking to those mounts, Travis."

"Some nice animals you have mounted there Mr. Hurley. Quite impressive, these been hunted around here?"

"Rocky Mountains mostly, that polecat was shot in the backyard, had killed a couple of calves, so I killed it. Ain't had any more problems with polecats since."

Chester Hurley sat down, lit a cigar, and offered one to each of them, only Tyrell and Riley accepted, Colby only shook his head 'no'.

"So, what brings workers from McCoy's all the way west?"

"We've been acquired by the law to track down a man- you have probably heard of him," Tyrell took a long pull on his cigar and exhaled. "We've been tracking Ski-be-nan-ted, you know who that is, don't you Mr. Hurley?"

"Please, call me Chester. Yes, I have heard of the Apache Kid. What makes Investigators think he's around here?"

"Witnesses mostly, and the fact, that we've been trailing him for some time. Haven't got close enough yet to confirm it, but we're certain it is him we've been trailing. Was identified by a couple of riverboat captains as being on their vessels, and one fellow at the Beacon Hill outpost, claimed to have seen a man on an Appaloosa, the same type of horse both riverboat captains saw," Tyrell took another plug off the cigar between his fingers.

"The Elquin Ranch west of here has Appaloosa's they're all branded though."

"The fella at Beacon Hill mentioned that, and said he noticed the brand on the Appaloosa he saw," Riley spoke up.

"Maybe it is one of the ranch hands from there?"

"It could be, Chester, but until we find out one way or the other, as far as we know it is the Apache Kid riding that Appaloosa."

"Hmmm, I heard he had been killed years ago."

"Many have said the same, but he is alive. And he's been seen in these parts, I can assure you of that."

"I ain't one to argue about something I ain't close too. Could be you are right. I wouldn't know. I do know none of us here have seen an Apache on a horse."

"You're far enough off the trail that he might have passed by without being seen," Colby said in response.

Bye now an old grey haired lady came out from the kitchen, with a pot of coffee on a silver tray, and she set it down on a table.

"Hello, I am Ruth Hurley. I have brought you coffee. I suppose my son has been talking your ears off. He is quite the chatterer once he gets talking. I am warming up some food for you, it should be ready soon," she looked at each of them and smiled.

"Nice to meet you Mrs. Hurley, and thank you for your hospitality and coffee, I'm Travis, this is Riley and Colby."

"Nice to meet each of you, too. Chester tells me that you work for McCoy's out of Fort Macleod."

"Yes, ma'am we do."

"I haven't been down east for a long time, my husband used to travel back and forth from there. While he was putting this place together, he worked at helping build the Fort. He probably built half of that town," Mrs. Hurley smiled as she reminisced about her late husband Chester Sr.

"He was one of the best engineers in these parts. Was often sought to help build start up towns, God bless his soul. How I miss him."

"Never mind, mother, don't get all weepy eyed. I'm sure our guests don't want to hear about what was."

"That is all right, Chester, we don't mind."

"Oh, the boy, doesn't like me talking about his father, I think it is because he misses him as much as I do. It is usually he, that gets all weepy eyed," Mrs. Hurley, tapped Chester on the shoulder as she looked at Travis and smiled. "They were both very close. Anyway, I will let you folks be, I have work to do in the kitchen." Turning she walked away.

"Sorry about that, sometimes mother talks about things that are irrelevant."

"You don't need to apologies, Chester. Sounds to me like your ma, misses her husband is all. Nothing wrong with that," Riley pointed out.

"So, you're pa was an engineer, eh?"

"He was. Built this place with his own two hands, pa could build anything, from wagon wheels to water mills. I don't know where he ever found the time to build some of the things he is accredited for building. It was a pastime for him, and every moment he could spare he was always building one thing or the other."

Chester chuckled as he thought about his father.

"He was an engineer and cattle rancher all at the same time, always kept busy. I myself find running eight hundred head or so of cattle leaves little time for anything else."

As darkness came and lanterns were lit, Mrs. Hurley offered cake and coffee before scooting off to bed. It was an added treat and complimented the meal that they had eaten a short while earlier. They indulged in the offering and conversed for a few hours, talking about this, that, and the other thing. Finally, Chester led them to a room where they were welcomed to lay out their bedrolls. The one bed in the room was given to Riley. Tyrell and Colby took places on the floor.

"Breakfast is served at the crack of dawn. I hope you will join us," Chester said as he bid them good night.

"You can bet on it, Chester, we'll be there."

Nodding, Chester closed the door and headed to his own bed.

Chapter 16

Early the next morning after having breakfast with the Hurley's, and thanking them for their hospitality once more, Tyrell, Riley, and Colby along with Black Dog headed west, their destination the Elquin Ranch, and miles of trail that lie ahead. That was January 9, 1892.

"It was quite a pleasant night at the Hurley's wasn't it?"

"Interesting people that is for sure, Riley, very kind, righteous, and hard working I'd say," Tyrell responded as they carried on.

"You figure we'll make the Elquin Ranch by day's end, Travis?"

"Depending on how things go, I don't see why we wouldn't. We've travelled ten or so miles already and it ain't even noon yet. We keep this pace up, I reckon we'll make the distance, Colby, or in the least be damn close."

Unknown to the three of them up ahead about three miles and coming out of the bush was a man on an Appaloosa, and strapped to a scabbard was an old .50 cal Hawken. The man had been hiding out in the mountains for the past few days, hungry and cold he had decided to continue with his journey into the Athabasca territory, the well-known warrior and his brother Crying Wolf he knew would give him sanctuary.

The southern Apache's were mostly all descendants of the northern Athabasca tribe, and the roots Ski-be-nan-ted had with them were deep. His escape from the Marshals that were taking him to prison years earlier for the murder of the man that had murdered his adopted father was said to be an impossible feat, and his legend grew from there.

During the escape, one of the three Marshals died. Although it was not Ski-be-nan-ted that killed the man, he was nonetheless, accused of that murder. That was when the rumors started that he was a ruthless killer, cattle rustler and the like, yet he was neither. He had been running for what seemed like eternity. In the white-man's world he knew he could never rest, and not until he hung from a rope would the white-man stop looking for him. For five years, he had managed to stay clear of the law, and for five years, his life had been nothing but hell. He wanted peace, he wanted to be forgotten to live in anonymity and the only place left on earth he knew where he would have a chance at that, was to live among the Athabasca and so that was his destination.

The three of them continued west at a slow canter, until finally they saw the trail of one rider that had travelled out of the bush and took up the trail they were on. They slowed their horses to a stop and looked around.

"Ain't no denying, someone came off those mountains and headed west here," Tyrell pointed out.

"It weren't too long ago either," Riley stated as he swung off his horse and looked closer to the trail left behind.

"I'd say these tracks, Travis, are as fresh as ours, someone is ahead of us. Think it might be the Kid?"

"It'd make sense wouldn't it? Who else would be up in those hills in the middle of winter," Colby stated as he now too stood next to Riley and looked at the trail coming out of the bush.

"Until we catch up we ain't going to know one way or the other. Let's ride," Tyrell said as he waited for both Colby and Riley to get back up on their horses. The three now galloped as they proceeded west. The trail they were following once more headed into the bramble in a northwesterly direction.

"Whoever is ahead has now headed into those mountains," Riley said as they stopped and looked on.

"Think we should follow?"

"I ain't sure that be our best bet, we didn't see who it might be. Could be a trapper, would hate like hell to waste time tracking someone in the mountains to only learn it ain't our man."

"It would be a damn shame if it was him and we didn't go looking."

"True as that is Colby, a single man on a horse in the mountains ain't going to stay in those mountains long. Not with the snow as deep as it likely is," Tyrell continued to look in the direction the trail led. Colby was right of course, they needed to know if it was Ski-be-nan-ted and the only way they'd ever know would be to follow.

"Damn it. I guess we best follow the trail. It turns out to be nothing, at least we'd know. All right, let's get," Tyrell said as he heeled his horse and the three of them along with Black Dog cut off the main trail and followed.

Ski-be-nan-ted had heard the riders approach while he was on the trail below and in a hasty move, he headed back into the mountains. He stood now on a ridge and looked back the way he had come, and sure enough, three men on horses were coming towards him.

He looked up the slope that was behind him, pulled his horse up to a tree, tossed his gear and Hawken into the bramble and out of sight. Then without dismounting, he jumped from his horse into the tree and climbed up some. Now clinging to the tree branches, he scooted the horse off, the horse headed directly back the way they had travelled. Ski-be-nan-ted, had done this trick many times, and it had worked well. He could only hope it worked this time too.

The sound of the horse crashing through the bush, caught the three riders off guard. Quickly they swung off their horses and drew their weapons waiting for what they thought to be an impending attack, but all that came from it was a single horse without a rider. Satisfied that no one was near, Colby slowly approached the horse and took it by the reins, it was indeed an Elquin Ranch branded Appaloosa.

"Shit, what do yous make of this?" he questioned as he led the horse back to where Tyrell and Riley stood.

"Goddamn, ain't sure what to make of it," Tyrell said as he looked the horse over. "Logic would depict the rider was thrown off, or has decided to head off on foot. I reckon we best follow the trail and see where it leads us."

Leading the Appaloosa the three continued following the trail, it led them up the mountain for a distance to where the horse had turned tail and headed back down. There were no footprints, or signs of anyone being thrown from a horse.

"Hmmm, this don't make much sense does it?" Riley said as he looked around.

"Nope, nope, it sure don't. There ain't no damn tracks of anyone on foot. We can see here where the horse turned tail and headed back down. I guess we need to follow the trail down, could be any rider might have been tossed off down some." Tyrell stroked his whiskered chin as he contemplated. Was it possible that there was no rider at all, or maybe the rider had been tossed off a few miles back and they had been following only the horse? With questions abound and the mystery unsolved. The three of them turned and followed the horses descending trail.

Ski-be-nan-ted squatted on a branch not making a sound as he watched the three men turn back and follow the trail that led back down the mountain.

He waited a few more minutes until the three riders had vanished from his view. Satisfied that they were gone, he swung out of the tree, gathered his gear, and followed close behind. On foot now, he knew he was vulnerable. He would find another horse there was no doubt about that, there were homesteads scattered here and there all throughout the area. As long as he used stealth and wit, finding another horse, was the least of his worries.

There were many miles to go before he would be in Athabasca territory. Once there, he knew he would be relatively safe, getting there was another story.

Finally making some distance down the mountain and not finding any rider or tracks of someone running off, the three of them stopped.

"Could be I reckon we've been following only the horse," Tyrell said as they looked back up the mountain, each wondering what it all meant.

"So, if there ain't no one about than that'd mean the rider might have got thrown or lost his horse back easterly some."

"Could be that is how it is, it's the only thing that makes sense."

"Shit, so we're going to have to go back, ain't we?"

"Let's get down onto the main trail first," Tyrell responded as he looked one last time up the mountain. Turning their horses the three of them made their way down to the main trail.

"What do you want to do, Travis?" Riley asked as they finally made the distance and pulled their horses to a stop.

"The only option I can come up with is that we need to head back east, pick up the trail that busted out of the bush and follow it some into the mountains, maybe we'll find a rider."

"I reckon that is the only option, it's going to slow us down a few hours, might not make the Elquin Ranch today after all."

"Nope, we might not, but we might have the Kid."

"No use debating anymore, let's ride," Colby said as the three of them turned back easterly.

It took an hour to make the distance back to where they had first discovered the trail. By now, Ski-be-nan-ted had made the distance to the main trail, and staying hidden, he looked west then east and smiled. His plan had worked. The three men had headed back east.

He had time now to put some distance between them. He darted through the bush with the stealth of a polecat, and agility of a rutting white tail buck. He'd stay in the undergrowth and work his way along the trail until he found another horse, gained back the Appaloosa, or the men passed him. Until then he would follow the main trail in the obscurity of the forest.

At the head of the first trail, Tyrell, Riley, and Colby, tethered the Appaloosa and leaving it a handful of grain, they turned into the bramble and followed the trail that had come off the mountain. It was tough going as they ascended. By mid afternoon they found no sign of a thrown rider, what they did find was a recent fire and lean-to. Swinging off their horses they looked around, it was obvious that someone had spent a few days there.

Colby stirred the ashes and was surprised to find below the deep ash a few embers still glowed.

"Whoever was here ain't been gone long, we got some hot coals still simmering. I'd say this fire burned all night and was stoked up in the morning."

Tyrell and Riley walked over and investigated.

"I'd say this fire ain't been out long, which adds a bit more confusion to this entire situation. If we ain't found a rider, means a rider ain't been thrown off. I ain't ever came across a scenario like this, what about you, Travis?"

Tyrell shook his head.

"Nope, can't say as I have Riley. You ever see anything like this, Colby?"

"I'm swinging from the same rope as you twos. It don't make a lick of sense to me none. I'd conclude though, that when that horse left here, it had a rider."

"That is my conclusion too, how about you, Riley, that your conclusion?"

"There ain't any other conclusion to conclude, I don't reckon. There ain't no one around, and we didn't find no rider. Only thing that makes sense is they rode out of here. The rest is a mystery."

"Or is it? If my mind serves me right, weren't where that horse turned back down from that last place we followed the trail to, near a few big trees?" Colby asked inquisitively.

"I didn't pay much attention, when I think about it though, I think it was," Tyrell said as he walked over to his horse.

"No, Colby is right that Appaloosa was next to a tree when it seemed to have turned back," Riley confirmed.

"That is what I thought too," Colby began, "I'm thinking maybe the Kid was in a tree."

"Jesus Christ, would have never even thought about that. That'd be why we didn't find no tracks, the son-of-a-bitch might have jumped from his horse into a damn tree. C'mon we have to get back there," Tyrell said as the three of them mounted up.

"That is a helluva thought you had there, Colby," Riley said as they headed back to the main trail.

"For the time being that is all it is, just a thought I had, if I'm right though, than the Kid sure pulled a fast one on us."

They rode in silence for a few minutes as they descended back onto the trail. Gathering the Appaloosa, they hurried back to where the trail led them back into the mountains. To keep their pace, Riley stayed on the main trail with the Appaloosa while Tyrell and Colby headed again back into the mountain. Sure enough as they grew closer, they could see that someone on foot headed down.

"Jesus, look at that Colby, your hunch was right. Whoever was riding that Appaloosa is on foot now. Let's follow their trail."

It led them only a short distance away from where Riley and the Appaloosa were held up.

"Hey, Riley!" Colby hollered, "Over here."

"I see yous!" Riley yelled back as he swung up onto his horse and led the Appaloosa to where Tyrell and Colby now stood.

"Colby was right, we found this trail, whoever was on that horse is on foot now, and they're heading west," Tyrell said as Riley approached.

"So, the son-of-a-bitch was in a tree?" Riley swung off his horse and walked over.

"Ain't sure he was in a tree, we spotted the tracks before we made the distance, but, he was certainly near when we first followed the trail."

Riley knelt down and looked at the tracks.

"Small feet, Apache I'd say, on foot he ain't going to be too far ahead, an hour or so walk might put him a couple miles west."

"Looks like, he's sticking close to the trail, walking through the bush. We ain't going to be able to follow him on horse through that bramble, he's heading west though, for now."

"What are we going to do?"

"A man without a horse is going to be looking for a horse. I figure we continue west for a few miles, then, when we figure we're ahead, we set up camp. We use that Appaloosa as bait. Chances are if we get ahead and he sees us, he's going to follow close behind, with hopes of getting his ride back."

"Goddamn, that might work, Travis," Riley said as he looked at him.

"It might, only way we'll know is to see what comes of it. I reckon if the rider of the Appaloosa is an hour ahead and on foot, he ain't too far away. He'll be watching the trail. C'mon, let's head up some, and set-up for the evening," Tyrell said as he and Colby waited for Riley to get back on his saddle.

"You all right there, Riley, getting up on that horse of yours?" Tyrell questioned.

"I'm fine," Riley said as he swung up, it hurt some, but he had felt worse pain in his time. The three of them along with Black Dog continued west along the trail. The Appaloosa led nicely and didn't hinder their trek much, Black Dog who was always vigilant, had taken notice to a new scent in the air. It was a human scent, and he stopped for a minute and scented the air.

"Hold up, there fellas. I think Black Dog has picked up a scent," Tyrell said as he slowed his horse and looked in the direction that Black Dog seemed to be looking. He saw nothing nor did the others, and Black Dog soon lost interest and carried onward.

"Must've been a deer or something, he ain't interested no more. I reckon we carry on another mile and then stop for the night. Let's get," Tyrell added as the three continued west.

Less than a mile later, they stumbled upon an old campsite that was off the trail a short distance, and decided to make it theirs for the evening. It didn't take long to make it cozy, and the three of them sat around the fire waiting for darkness to come, and a possible intruder looking for a horse.

"You think back there a ways, when your dog stopped, that he might have scented the Kid, Travis?"

"Could be he did. I reckon that would've been the distance a man could've made running through the bush on foot. Don't know why he lost interest though," Tyrell shrugged.

"If it were the Kid, he'd be getting close to us by now. Let's hope he comes for his horse, 'cause I ain't one to look forward to traipsing through the bush looking for someone we ain't even sure is who it is we are looking for," Riley burbled, he had got into the last of his whisky shortly after they had stopped and set up their camp. It was all he could do to force away the pain he was now experiencing.

"I figure you're a couple of sandwiches short a picnic basket, Riley. Who else do you think would've been riding that Appaloosa?" Colby questioned with a chuckle.

"If it is the Kid, why the hell ain't he come for his horse, yet?" Riley swayed a bit and looked again into the fire. He was numb, nothing made sense, decapitated bodies, frozen men, horses without riders, riverboats, and the one that pissed him off most, his ruined shirt and jacket. With one last swig from the whisky bottle, he fell over and passed out.

"Jesus Christ, c'mon, Colby give me a hand here, let's get old Riley wrapped up at least, the son-of-a-bitch is drunk."

The two of them wrestled with his limp body until finally getting him covered up so that he wouldn't freeze to death. Adding more wood to the fire the frozen piece hissed and sizzled as the flame took away the moisture and the wood finally began to burn.

"There that brings up the flames. I think tonight it's going to be colder than last."

"Every night is a cold one out on the trail and especially in mid of winter."

"I don't suppose that could be argued none," Colby leaned forward and warmed his hands as he looked into the flames.

The two of them, while Riley slept, wrapped themselves up in their blankets and huddled close to the fire. The silence of growing darkness brought with it a clear and starry sky. A cold wind blew every now and again making the flames of their fire flicker this way and that.

Tyrell looked across the fire to Colby.

"Tell me, Colby," he began, "how do you like the job so far?"

"It ain't nothing I don't reckon, that is different from anything else one might do. You do what you have to, Travis. Make do with what you got, and know why it is you're doing it in the first place. Everything else that comes along, comes with what it is one does."

Tyrell wrapped his blanket around his shoulders tighter and nodded.

"That is a mighty fine outlook, and I reckon, even some wisdom in there. You keep thinking like that, Colby, in all that you do in life. Yes sir."

He felt a new kind of respect for him. He had thought that by now Colby would have been tired of all that had gone on, but that certainly wasn't the case. If anything, Colby it seemed had found his true calling. Tyrell smiled.

"And you, what about you. You ain't been in this business long," Colby asked with honesty.

"Nope, I sure haven't. I was kind of hooked into it, in a sense."

"Oh, how is that?"

"Long story actually."

"I don't mind a bit of history, long stories is good around a fire."

Tyrell nodded and looked into the flames, then back to Colby and he proceeded to tell the tale on how he first met Ed and had given him a second horse he had. How he then worked for Mac and eventually made his way to the Fort to gather the horse he leant Ed, and at the same time take him up on his offer of employment.

"So, just like that you started working for McCoy's?"

"Just like that, yep."

"How long now you been working for them?"

"It certainly ain't as long as it seems, it'll be a whole of one year this June I reckon."

"Huh, I thought it was a hell of a lot longer than that."

Tyrell shook his head, "nope, one year in June. Like I said earlier, it seems a lot longer than it is. I reckon I have spent most of it on the trail of one bounty or the next. Seems never ending to be truthful," Tyrell once more turned his gaze to the fire and looked on.

"You reckon you'll still be with McCoy's come this June, Travis?"

"I don't see why not. I like the job, the folks I work with. I make a living, but risk a lot, life and limb come to mind. I ain't sure one or the other equal good fortune, or, good luck. I ain't died yet, ain't been shot. So, I'd say I've had good luck, money don't mean much if one is dead."

"Nor does luck," Colby said with a chuckle, as the two of them grew silent deep in thought.

With at least an hour of daylight left Ski-be-nan-ted kept up his stride of both jogging and running. The snow hampered him some and made things difficult, slipping and sliding as he continued his gait, sweat ran down his squared jawed face and he stopped briefly to wipe it away. To sweat as he was, he knew, would only bring on a more disastrous out-come than trying to avoid three men on horses. With the clothes he wore, he knew he was vulnerable to hypothermia, and that is exactly what would happen if he continued to run and sweat.

Inhaling deeply he sighed. Here he was in the cold of winter, without a horse, food or drier clothes. What he wore was all he had, and it consisted of nothing more than an old pair of moccasins, his black felt jacket, denim pants, hat, and the buckskin clothes he wore beneath. Around his waist, he had a skinning knife and hatchet, grasped in his hand was his old .50 caliber Hawken.

He shivered as the cold bit at his sweaty damp body. For now he would walk. Standing he trudged onward, the snow was knee deep and with every step he took his freezing feet ached with pain. Soon he knew he would have no choice but to stop and light a fire. He could only hope that the three men were fooled by his attempt to avoid them. He wished now that he hadn't even tried. He couldn't be sure who they were, although his instincts told him, that the three men were looking for the Apache Kid a name he had grown to hate. The rumors and hearsays had given him that name, he had lived with it for too long, and certainly not by choice.

He stopped now as he looked toward the trail. He could see the flickering flames of a fire from where he stood, he couldn't see much of anything else, but he did know it could be his opportunity to gather a horse, fires had men and men had horses. In stealthy silence he made his way toward the flames, the only sound was that of the wind that occasionally blew tousling the branches of trees to and fro.

Now in viewing distance he could see two men huddled near a fire with woolen blankets draped across their shoulders. He saw nothing else and he looked on with intent. Then, within a heartbeat, an unseen assailant wrestled him to the ground. He struggled some until he realized who it was that had him in their grip. It was Crying Wolf.

"Sshhh, keep quiet, Ski-be-nan-ted. It is I Crying Wolf."

"Yes, I see that now," Ski-be-nan-ted, said as Crying Wolf gently released him.

"Follow me, quickly."

The two of them stood up and darted a short distance to where Crying Wolf had two horses tethered.

"We can talk now."

"How did you know, I was coming this way?"

"You are a wanted Indian, wanted Indians always come back to their roots," Crying Wolf said as he embraced Ski-be-nan-ted. "You look, ah, not bad," he smiled. "Come, I have a camp not far from here," Crying Wolf said as the two of them jumped up onto a horse each. Not even their horses it seemed made a sound as the two riders cautiously cut up an old trail and into the high country. A few minutes later, they were at Crying Wolf's camp.

"Here is home for now."

Crying Wolf slid off his horse and made his way to the small fire that gently flickered followed by Ski-be-nan-ted.

"You have been on the trail a long time Ski-be-nan-ted, you must be weary."

"Yes, I am cold and weary," he said as he sat down and warmed himself.

Crying Wolf handed him a cup of tea.

"Drink this. I will make food."

"Yes, yes, thank you my brother," Ski-be-nan-ted huddled closer to the fire as Crying Wolf roasted a hare over the flames.

"The men below. I know them, and yes they are looking for Ski-be-nan-ted, the Apache Kid."

"I assumed that, from the beginning. They have my horse."

"It is that horse, Ski-be-nan-ted that brought them to you. Haven't our ways taught you not to steal branded horses?"

Crying Wolf smiled as he now tore the roasted hare in half and handed one-half to Ski-be-nan-ted.

"Ah, it matters not, you are safe now, and we have two unbranded horses."

Ski-be-nan-ted looked across the fire and smiled.

"Yes, and we are with blood."

"Tell me, Ski-be-nan-ted, you have taken many years to come back home. Was the white man's world so appealing?"

"I am hated by many of us, from the prairie to the dry lands of the new Apache. I have been hunted by my kind, and the white man; for a long time my brother. To stay away from my true home protected my kin. Now, many more years have come and gone, and I am still hated by most."

"You must understand why."

"Yes. Let it be known, that I, Ski-be-nan-ted was an Apache Scout who tried to bring peace and prosperity to the land of the Indian, forced by the U.S.A, and their lawmakers to track Geronimo. When the white man no longer needed my help, they accused me of murder. Yet, I was innocent, and sent to a white man's prison, many miles from the land of my father. The two men, who died when the opportunity to make my escape came, were not killed by my hand. Yet again, I was accused of that too. My life after that was not by choice but of necessity to stay alive. To see my home again and make peace with my people."

"As your kin, Ski-be-nan-ted, I know this, and it is why I am here now. Our people, the Athabasca understand this. You are not hated by us and have been missed and longed for by many, your return is good medicine."

"I have killed men that were bad, they steal from their own kind, and I protected the white man from loss of their livelihood, yet many white men still want to hang me. The white man's world is far from appealing, Crying Wolf."

The two men looked up to the heavens and the flickering stars as the snow began to fall.

"There will be much snow this night. Our tracks, yours, and mine will be hidden. The white men below will not follow us," Crying Wolf said as he now looked into the flames of their small fire, and warmed his hands. As darkness settled in, the two men wrapped themselves up with Indian blankets and talked softly amongst themselves.

"How do you know the white men below?" Ski-be-nan-ted, asked.

"They are friends, the one man Travis saved my life some weeks ago, after I put to death the bad man Gabe Roy."

"I am glad to hear that man is dead. I am proud to know it was my brother that killed him."

"I could not leave that place Willow Gate, while I knew he lived. I have avenged our brother and niece. I am at peace now, knowing he is dead."

Crying Wolf wrapped his blanket around his shoulders and smiled.

"Yes, I am at peace, our brother and his daughter can now leave this place and join the great Indian warriors and women that have died at the hands of the white man."

Chapter 17

It was early morning when the three men rose. To their surprise, the Appaloosa remained tethered.

"It don't look like the Kid came back for his horse," Riley said as he stirred the coals and added more wood to their fire.

"I see that, and this damn snow will have certainly covered any tracks we might have been able to find."

"What do we do now, Travis?" Colby asked as he poured a morning coffee.

"I don't know, we were so damn close, now, I don't think we'll ever be that close again. The Kid didn't come for his horse as I first thought he would have. A man on foot can certainly travel through areas where men on horses can't go. We might as well be looking for a three sided coin," Tyrell replied as though in defeat.

"Any man traipsing through these woods at this time of year is still going to be looking for a horse, no man in his right mind wouldn't be."

"What are you saying?"

"I figure the Kid is still going to be looking for a horse. There has to be a ranch or two around here somewhere that has horses. Maybe we'll get lucky as we carry onward and find one that has had a horse stolen. Besides we have a branded Appaloosa that since it is in our possession needs to be returned, regardless," Riley pointed out.

"You want us to carry on to the Elquin Ranch, to return a stolen horse?"

"The horse belongs to them, Colby."

"Sure it does, but we ain't supposed to care about a horse, we is looking for the Apache Kid, Ski-be-nan-ted, have you forgotten that Riley? I don't reckon he could have got far, he's walking for Christ Sake, and it snowed like a son-of-a-bitch last night and was damn cold. He had to have stopped and lit a fire somewhere, all we need to do is find that spot.”

“I ain’t forgotten, I know who it is we have been commissioned to find. We can’t simply turn that Appaloosa loose and not worry about it. This damn snow will have hampered any tracks that we may have been able to find, and leading a horse you can bet will slow us down a great deal in making any progress.”

“You well enough to carry on alone, Riley?”

Riley looked up to Tyrell and nodded.

“Am so. You want me to carry on whilst; you two head back to see if you can pick up the Kid’s trail, don’t ya?”

“It is a viable solution. We’ll circle back around and I reckon we could catch up with you later today, as long as you don’t wander off the trail. We might get a lead on where the Kid went next.”

Riley inhaled deeply and shook his head.

“Look around, Travis; you see our tracks from last night?”

“Nope, nope, I sure don’t.”

“Well, that is what you’ll be looking for if you two head back.”

“So, what do you suggest?”

“We carry on. As I said there has to be a ranch around here or homestead, the Kid is going to be looking for a horse. He ain’t going to want to walk. Not while he is on the run. He’s a fugitive, and he’s going to try to get as far away from us as he can get in the shortest amount of time, and even more so now that it snowed. He knows his tracks will be covered.”

Colby and Tyrell looked at each other and shook their heads, Riley was right of course.

“Jesus Christ, Riley, you and your Goddamn logic,” Tyrell said as he and Colby sat back down.

"What if there ain't no places for miles that has horses, what then? If we don't come across a trail of a single man on foot, or go looking for it we'll never catch the Kid then," Colby pointed out.

As if it were his cue, Black Dog looked into the forest on the other side of the trail and strutted off. The three of them simply assumed he was taking off to have a crap somewhere, and they continued to bicker back and forth on what to do next. It was, while they were loading up their gear that Tyrell took notice that Black Dog hadn't yet returned.

"Shit, I wonder where that damn dog got to," he said as he and the others looked around. He called him a few times and still there was no sign of him.

"You reckon he might have scented something, maybe the Kid?"

"There is a good chance he scented something, ain't sure what, but, he don't usually stay away this long without reason."

Tyrell swung up onto his horse.

"I'm going to follow his trail, and give him a call up yon some, I lost him once, I'll be damned if I'm going to lose him again."

Colby and Riley waited for what seemed like eternity, they could hear Tyrell calling the dog and each time they heard him he was getting more distant.

"Goddamn it. Can't even hear him anymore."

The two of them were getting anxious and concerned when finally they saw him trotting back with no dog trailing behind.

"It don't look like he's got that dog of his with him," Riley said as the two looked on and waited for him to approach. A few minutes later, Tyrell pulled up.

"I think Black Dog has picked up the Kid's trail, he's following something or someone that headed into the high country. I came across a definite trail. I'd say it is new, likely from last night. The dog ain't coming though when I call him, so, I'm going to follow him."

"What about us, what are we supposed to do?"

"You and Riley stick to his advice, carry on down the main trail, I'll catch up with yous. If I spot the Kid or…"

Riley interrupted him there.

"Hold on, there is that dog of yours now," he said as Tyrell turned in his saddle and looked back. He turned his horse so he could have a better view of Black Dog, there was something dangling from his mouth he noticed.

"He's got something," Tyrell mentioned as he swung off his horse and waited for the dog.

Black Dog approached and dropped on the ground the charred carcass of a rabbit.

"Jesus look at that, looks like somebody's supper from last night. Good boy, Black Dog." Tyrell scratched him behind the ear.

"That there is the proof that we need, we follow Black Dog's trail it'll leads us to where someone had a fire and spent the night. I'd bet a year of wages that it was the Kid."

"I wouldn't argue that none. How far up in the hills do you figure that dog went to find that?" Colby questioned.

Tyrell shook his head.

"It can't be more than a mile or so, I don't reckon."

"That certainly brightness up my day, we got a half ass chance now," Riley mentioned as the three swung up onto their horses.

Taking the Appaloosa by its reins, they set off to follow the trail that Black Dog had laid out for them. It took less than an hour to find the camp, the only problem was, two people wearing moccasins and two horses had spent the night there.

They swung off their horses and looked around. Tyrell was filled with disappointment. What they had come across was an overnight camp of two men.

"What are the odds that this camp ain't what we hoped it to be? But a Goddamn two man camp," Tyrell sighed.

Riley squatted as he looked around.

"I ain't so sure that is all it is, Travis. The Blood, Blackfoot, and Athabasca ain't going to be this far west at this time of year, two, of one or the other were here though, the tracks tell us that. They left early morn' and headed northwesterly."

Riley looked in that direction and contemplated.

"The question I think we need to ask; is why, were they here," he added.

"Maybe they was jus' out hunting or something, shit there could be a number of reasons why two Indians would be out and about. We is looking for one, not two. It is damn confusing is what it is."

"Can we look at this as a coincidence though?"

"No, bloody way is this a coincidence," Riley shook his head, he was certain of that.

"Well, if it ain't a coincidence, then what the hell are we looking at Riley?"

"I think someone other than us has found the Kid. I figure they had an extra horse with them for that reason, likely had a prearranged meeting point along the trail below."

"You think one of the two which spent the night here was the Kid?"

Riley nodded.

"I don't believe it to be a coincidence, a prearranged meeting seems more likely to me."

"All we can do it that case is follow this trail, and see who or where it brings us."

"I reckon so, and leading this extra horse is going to be a pain in the backside."

"We'll take turns leading it, no worries there, Riley. I guess we carry on from here, then," Tyrell sucked on an eyetooth as he looked around one last time and the three of them mounted up. Heeling their horses they followed the trail that lead northwesterly.

Crying Wolf and Ski-be-nan-ted, who were some miles away slowed their horses to a stop so they could rest.

"We grow closer to the Athabasca territory, in two days we will be home."

"It has been a long time since I smelled the beauty of this place," Ski-be-nan-ted inhaled deeply.

The scents, the beauty, he had missed it all.

"The forest and beauty has not changed from the memories I have held onto, how was it that you found me?"

"I listened to the wind, heard the voices of white men who spoke of you. They are not all wise, they leave behind clues and words to others and if one listens, it is not hard to learn what they will do next. From what I learned and heard I conjured visions on where you would be and from those visions came our reunion."

"You have always believed and followed your visions. Many though from memory failed you. I am glad you have continued to believe, perhaps if you hadn't our reunion would not have taken place yet, and I may have died at the hands of those that track me."

"No. Those white men tracking you, would not have killed you, they would have kept you alive and brought you before their laws."

"This is the same as death."

"Let us not talk about that, Ski-be-nan-ted, but of your renewed life. It is not your time to die."

"Yes, you are right, Crying Wolf. Come let us continue now with our journey. I sense more snow coming."

Turning their horses, they continued on, and rode in silence.

By midday another snowstorm swept across the mountains. The whistling wind brought on whiteout conditions, and both parties travelling northwesterly were forced to stop and seek refuge from the impending snowstorm.

"Goddamn, we better head into the trees and get out of this damn wind and snow," Tyrell yelled as the wind picked up and the fast falling snow stung their eyes. Leading the Appaloosa, he and Black Dog headed into the undergrowth and found an area out of the wind and snow. Followed close behind by Riley and Colby, the three of them dismounted and tethered their rides and extra horse.

"We ought to get a shelter up; I don't think this snow is going to let up for a while. We best prepare for the worst," Tyrell said.

The three men began the task of building a lean-to and gathering wood, it took some time to finish the task. Finally, it was done and during that time, the snow fell from the sky constant and fast and it continued to fall now.

"Can't even see the sky, she's coming down hard," Colby said above the wind as the three of them tucked into their quickly built shelter. It kept the snow off and wind at bay, but the cold bit at them relentlessly. Even wrapped up in their bedrolls and heavy felt jackets the cold penetrated every bone in their bodies. All they could do was hope that the wind died down soon so that they could light a fire.

They shivered and shook as they waited and talked. It seemed like hours before the wind finally slowed. It had no effect on the falling snow though and it continued to fall blanketing the mountains and their surroundings. No longer could they even see their trail, it, and the trail they had been following had been obliterated by the freshly fallen snow.

"There ain't no way we're leaving here yet. We best get a fire going and gather more cedar boughs to block off the cold now that the wind has stopped."

"You got that right, Riley. I reckon we're stuck here for the night and it's going to be dark soon."

Stepping out of their crudely built shelter they trampled the snow down where they would light a fire, Riley was left with that task while Tyrell and Colby gathered cedar boughs and draped them over the entrance to their shelter. Using their hands and the small prospecting shovel that Riley always carried, they tossed snow over the entire thing. Inside they built a smaller fire pit, leaving an opening in the snow-covered shelter for smoke to escape.

The outside fire was now lit, and they removed their horse saddles and set them down around it so they had something to sit on. Wrapping themselves up with the horse blankets and bedrolls, they sat solemnly around the fire and waited the storm out.

"It sure came on quick, didn't it?"

"It did indeed, ruined any chance of us following that trail too," Riley mentioned as he added another piece of wood to the fire.

"We know which way they was going, I reckon they've been held up by the storm too, so, not all has been lost yet, Riley. I think we still have a chance at finding their trail."

"That would depend on how far they managed since morning, and how lucky we get, Travis. Shit, she snowed for a few hours already and it ain't lightened up. We can't even see our own damn trail anymore, she's buried," Colby commented.

Tyrell looked back the way they had come and nodded.

"No matter what, we need to make it off this mountain and when we do we'll travel in the direction we know the two riders went. Black Dog might be able to steer us right. If it does turn out we've lost the trail, well then, we'll have to reevaluate the situation."

As the darkness of evening enveloped them and the winter storm moved on, the sound of a gunshot echoed to the south, it startled them and they dove for cover. In quick succession, another round of shots pierced the evening calm. The gunshots then they could tell were a distance away. They were not in harm's way.

"What the hell do yous suppose that was all about?"

"As you'd say Colby, we're hanging from the same rope as you. I ain't sure what that was all about. I know it is too far away for us to be concerned," Tyrell looked southerly. His first thought was that the maniac Alvin had been found by his brother. The probability of that however was slim. Hell, the man they had met claiming to be Alvin's brother had travelled in the opposite direction and that was days ago already and miles away.

Next, he figured it could have been a few drunkards firing into the darkness in a drunken stupor, like what drunk men often do, he had done that himself on a few occasions. One thing was for certain, the shots fired weren't from a .50 caliber Hawken.

"Stuff like that in the darkness of evening in the middle of nowhere, in January sure makes a man wonder, don't it," Riley mentioned as he made his way back to the fire and sat down.

Colby and Tyrell were about to do the same thing when once again shots echoed in the distance, closer this time than last. The three of them pulled their weapons. Colby kicked snow over the glowing flames of their fire, as they sought cover. Whatever it was that was going on, the three of them were about to become a part of it. They had nowhere to go. They had no choice but to face whatever it was that was coming their way.

More shots echoed and the anguishing screaming of a man followed. From the forest a frightened horse bust out of the bush startling their own horses and all hell broke loose, Riley, able to catch the loose horse gained control of it, as Tyrell and Colby darted over to where their horses were tethered and settled them. The whole incident lasted less than a few minutes, and when order was finally restored, the horse Riley had in his clutches was covered in blood, yet it alone had no wounds.

Suddenly, from the direction of which the horse came, a blood soaked man appeared from within the shadows, a pistol in his hand and he pointed it and fired at nothing, then fell to the ground. Tyrell made his way near, his own pistol in his hand and ready to fire if need be. He knelt down and looked on. The man on the ground in front of him had parts and pieces missing. Riddled with a dozen or more bullets, he was lifeless.

By now both Colby and Riley were standing next to him, they looked on in awe as much as Tyrell continued his gaze. Their viewing and comprehension on what had taken place was interrupted by the sound of horse hooves. Armed still as the three were, they pointed their weapons as the voice of a man sounded in the shadows.

"Where the hell are you, Alvin? I know I didn't miss, you unholy son-of-a-bitch!" Finally, the man broke out of the bush and stopped abruptly when he realized, three weapons were pointing at him.

"Evening, gentlemen," he said as the three of them lowered their guns and put them away.

"So, this is Alvin?"

"It is what used to be Alvin, yes sir," the man said as he swung off his horse, and made the distance to where his brother's motionless body finally came to rest, he knelt next to it and shook his head.

"It took a dozen shots to drop the monster. Any man created by God would have fallen from the first. Like I told you three before, Alvin, he ain't right. He was a monster, plain and simple. The world can rest easy now."

The man began to stand when a glint of life glowed once more in Alvin, and in that brief second as though the will to kill and defy death, was his objective; Alvin pointed his pistol and fired the last round into his brother's face! At the same instant, Colby drew his own pistol and planted a bullet between the eyes of Alvin, before Alvin's brother even hit the ground. It was that quick and sudden. The fresh virgin snow glistened crimson from the blood and brain matter that exploded, and spilled out from the back and top of Alvin's head.

Colby looked on in shock for a moment, then, turning quickly he leaned against a tree and vomited. Riley and Tyrell stood in disbelief, both at how quickly Colby pulled his pistol and fired, and what had just taken place.

"You all right, Colby?"

"Sure, ain't nothing like seeing a man riddled with bullets up close, and then… and then, having to shoot him again. No, I'm fine Travis."

"You did the right thing. The bastard may have had enough life left to shoot one of us. Don't feel bad about what you did Colby."

"I don't feel badly at all, Riley. Just never seen a man with so many holes in him, nor have I seen a man's head explode. I'd rather have shot him from a distance, don't see so much then. I knew there was a reason I didn't like pistols."

"That aside, we have a brand new list of problems."

Tyrell moved over to where Alvin's brother lay on the ground, and he checked for a pulse.

"Nope, this one ain't breathing none either."

"Shit, like I said a few days ago, everyone keeps throwing rocks at us. What the hell are we going to do with two dead men and two more damn horses?"

"I don't know, Riley. The law needs to be informed that Alvin is dead, and so is his brother."

Tyrell looked around for the two horses the men had been riding; they were a distance away and obviously quite skittish.

"We'll have to coax those horses back, toss these bodies over their backs and head for the nearest town. Goddamn, slowed down again by the unexpected," Tyrell stood up and shook his head.

"Hindrance, goddamn hindrance," Riley said as he made his way closer to the two horses and tried to coax them in. It took a bucket of oats and almost an hour, but finally the two horses Alvin and his brother were riding were tethered.

"There we go three horses and two dead men. Come morning we're going to have to decide if we should turn back here, and head back to Beacon Hill, from there we can get word to the Mounties in Clear Water. Or lead the horses and the dead to the next town," Riley sighed as he sat down.

From the light of their fire now that it was alit once more, Tyrell, looked at the map.

"Ain't sure if following the two riders, one of which we think is the Kid is viable now. More important I think to let the law know about what took place here tonight. I reckon if we head back to Beacon Hill, we'd be able to give up that Appaloosa too. The law can deal with it."

"Yous two is saying we head back the way we came, hand over that Alvin fella and his brother and the Appaloosa to the redcoats, which are in Clear Water."

"Well, I can tell you, Colby, the nearest town is Beacon Hill. We know they have a telegraph office. I'd much rather head back then lead three horses and two dead men for three or four days before the next town. This way, we can be back on the trail the day after tomorrow, without the encumbrance of leading horses and the stink that will follow of two dead men."

"Goddamn it. We is pretty close to those we've been tracking, shit, if one of them two riders is the Kid, we'd be done with this job. The damn storm that passed through has likely slowed them down as we've said. They could be over the next hill, for Christ sakes."

"Could be, but, we ain't going to know which way they even went after here, we know the direction that is all."

"Why can't we kick these horses in the ass and send them running, they'd be found soon enough. You've done that before, with the Tellman brothers, this ain't no different."

"The Tellman brothers drew on me Colby; it was my life that was threatened. This here is different. Alvin, there, he is an escaped mental patient, and likely still being looked for. The man that filled him with all those holes is a man that claimed to be his brother, he attempted to kill Alvin and Alvin killed him. I'd say that there is the difference."

Colby shook his head as he looked into the flames. He knew Tyrell was right.

"Truth is, we don't have to like what needs to be doing, but, we have to do it. We have to turn Alvin and his brother over to the law, and the closest communication we can get with the law is at Beacon Hill. Likely there is an undertaker there as well, and a cold box for the dead."

"Why couldn't you and Riley head back to the Hill, I ain't got issue with carrying on alone for a couple of days. Yous would catch up."

Tyrell and Riley looked at each other, not sure if letting Colby go on alone was a wise decision or not.

"Quit looking at each other as though neither of yous knows how to answer. It s a simple question, and I'm well aware of the potential hazards which may be involved. I won't do a damn thing though other than track them two riders ahead of us. I'd wait for yous."

"You sure you want to do that Colby?"

"Why the hell not?" Colby questioned. "If one of us don't carry on following what we can of the trail, in two days when we make our way back here, shit, there'll be no sign of those we've been tracking. I got all the gear and whatnot I'd need."

"Damn it, Colby. I don't know, and it ain't because I don't think you can't manage, I just ain't sure of the risk."

"Like I said, Riley, I'll only track them, and yous two can track me, I'll be sure to keep my trail visible, follow it and yous would catch up, and we'd still be fresh on their trail then. We leave it for two or three days, I reckon there'd be no point, and we might as well turn back to the Fort."

"I don't know. What do you think, Travis?"

"Colby brings up some good points," Tyrell looked over to Colby who was looking back waiting for an answer.

"If you think that is something you want to do Colby, well then, I don't reckon we can argue the points you made. So, I say in the morning we'll head back to Beacon Hill, and you carry onward, try to pick up the trail we was following, and make damn certain you make your trail easy for us to find, so we can catch up. If things go awry head back this way and we'll catch up sooner."

"I'd agree to that," Colby nodded.

"All right, that is how it'll be then."

Conversing for a while longer and making sure each of them knew the risk of Colby going on alone, and what he would do if things went sideways, they tossed more wood on the fire and headed inside their crudely built shelter. That was the evening of January 10.

Chapter 18

On the morning of the 11th, before Tyrell and Riley headed back to Beacon Hill, Tyrell had Black Dog stay with Colby. Although Colby didn't think there was a need for that, he eventually relented.

"He'll keep you company for the time being if nothing else."

"I reckon there is more of a reason that you'd leave your dog with me. But, that is all right, if'n it'll make the two of you feel better that he tags alongside me, then I ain't going to argue about it," Colby took the last swallow of his morning coffee and gathered his gear.

"You be careful, Colby. Those you is following ain't your average bounty. They is Apache and they ain't going to be easy to track, as we've witnessed," Riley said as he stood next to Colby and his horse.

"They is still men, Riley, they tire, they eat, and they light fires and bleed like any of us."

"They've also been living in these parts for their entire lives and have adapted to anything mother earth throws at them. They're as coy and agile as the animals they hunt, never underestimate those that were here before us. That would be a death sentence," Riley pointed out with both authority and sincerity.

Neither he nor Tyrell wanted anything to happen to Colby, they both knew those he would tracking, didn't live by what they called civil laws. There were no second chances if one were to cross them, even if there were only two.

"I think I hear a bit of hesitation in your voice Riley. I know what it is that is expected of me, and I already told yous both, I ain't got no intentions on trying to bring the Kid in alone. All I'm going to do is follow. That is it. I can't however know what Travis' dog may or may not do, I'm hoping he don't give me up."

"No worries there. If you ain't in trouble, he ain't going to cause you none, I assure you of that, nor will he give you up. He'll stick to you, if something does come about, tell him to 'alert and guard' and that is exactly what he'll do," Tyrell assured, "his instincts take over after that."

Colby nodded.

"All right. Well, I'm set, got my gear and beans," he turned his horse in the direction he would be going. Looking back he smiled, tilted his hat and heeled his horse, "I'll be seeing yous in the coming days, keep your eyes peeled for oddities along my trail and you'll find me," he said as he and Black Dog headed northerly.

"There he goes, Travis. You reckon he'll be okay?"

"I'm most certain of it. He grabbed the bull by its sack, takes a fearless and willing man to do that alone," Tyrell chuckled at his own joke. "I think Colby knows what he's doing, he ain't stupid by any means, a little cocky at times but that is due to his adolescence. I think he's found his calling. I had words with him back on the trail some, he likes this job."

"I saw that in him too," Riley sighed. "I reckon you and I should get a move on to, Beacon Hill is a day's ride."

"Yes sir, and the sooner we get our doings done the sooner we can catch up to Colby."

Gathering their gear and looking around one last time for landmarks, they could easily remember the two of the headed back to the main trail and onward to Beacon Hill, toting along with them two dead men and three horses. The snow from the night before got less deep the closer they got to the main trail, and the easier it was for them as they travelled.

Colby on the other hand stayed up high for the first while until finally he came across an evening camp, and like the first, two men wearing moccasins, had spent the night there. He stirred the coals of what remained of the fire, but no coals glowed. He knew then that whoever had been there had at least a two or three hour head start and had left early that morning.

"Well, dog, looks like we has found what it is we needed to find. Shouldn't be too hard following now," he said to Black Dog who was sitting near. After relieving himself in a clump of trees, Colby broke some branches off and stuck them in the snow as to let Travis and Riley know that he was there. Then swinging back onto his horse he and Black Dog continued at a steady pace. The sun by now was a yellow ball in the sky and had warmed things up.

Colby squinted as he looked up to it to make a guess at what time of day it might have been. He guessed it was high noon. A few hours later, the trail he had been following now headed due west and deeper into the Columbia Mountains. He slowed his horse down and swung off. It was time to rest and mark the trail for a fifth time. He laid out three long branches in the shape of an arrow on top of the snow. Finished with that, he grabbed his canteen and took a drink, wiping his shirtsleeve across his mouth he leaned against his horse and looked on.

The day had been warm considering how the evening before had been, and he had managed to keep up the pace, but, by now was beginning to tire out. It was likely the two men he was following were in the mountains by then. Noting it would be getting onto dusk soon, he decided he'd push himself for another hour or so, and then settle for the evening.

Crying Wolf and Ski-be-nan-ted had made the distance to one of the Athabasca hunting grounds and they stopped for the evening.

"We will rest here tonight, Ski-be-nan-ted."

"Here is good. As a young child, I hunted here many times. It is the mountain of the skunk bear and brother moose."

"Since that time, many of the animals we hunted on this mountain have been trapped or killed by the white man. Their greed has diminished the numbers that were here when we were young."

"It is the same everywhere. Greed is a vicious disease very prominent in the white man. That is their weakness."

Crying Wolf nodded in agreement.

"The white man have many things that corrupt them, greed, yes, is one of them."

The two men went about gathering wood for their fire and packing down the snow where they would sit and sleep. With the task finished and flames from their fire flickering, they sipped rose pedal tea.

"Do you think those that were tracking me, continue to do so?"

"Yes. For now they have been slowed down by last evening's storm," Crying Wolf looked to the sky, "and tonight there will be no storm, they will gain distance as the days come. But, we will be home soon enough," he took a swallow from the cup in his hand.

"We will leave this place in the early twilight of the new day. Perhaps, we can travel further if we go through the swamp lands, they will be froze," Ski-be-nan-ted suggested as he sipped his tea.

"It is perilous to travel that way, Ski-be-nan-ted. The snow that has fallen would make it difficult to navigate."

"It would slow down those that follow me."

"It would, yes, but as I said those following you are friends of such. I do not wish death upon them."

"I am confused by your words, Crying Wolf. You would not wish death upon them, but, you would be not so willing to stop them from following one of your kin from being captured and put to death by them?"

"If I had to make a choice, I would choose my kin. That is the Athabasca way. Do not fear that I wouldn't help my kin from being captured. It is my hope that we will not be faced with a confrontation. They do not know that it is I, who travels with you. I lied to them when we departed our ways weeks ago, that you, Ski-be-nan-ted, were not welcomed by the Athabasca. That we would not offer you sanctuary. If they catch up before we are home, I will convince them that you are not who they seek."

"How will you do that? They have seen my face on paper pictures."

"True as that may be, those pictures are old. You do not look so much like that man anymore."

"Perhaps. So who might I be?"

"We will say your name is Three Wolves Running."

"That is the name of our brother, the great Apache Warrior."

"Yes, but they do not know our brother's name. His spirit will come to you, if the white man catches up."

"How do you know this?"

"We have spoken. He came into my dreams two nights before I found you. He plotted the plan in my vision, and said 'bring Ski-be-nan-ted, home, my name will protect him,' that is what he spoke to me."

"It would not explain why the two of us are here, so close to where I fooled the white man and let my horse go. If they find our trail, they will not think it to be a coincidence. They will be quick to judge that who they follow is I and a friend."

"Yes, and we will convince them otherwise, or, there will be bloodshed. But, only then will I raise my bow."

"To travel through the swamps land would prevent such a possible confrontation."

"They would know that any Indian travelling through such an unsafe place, would only be one that is on the run. We stay on our course through the Columbia Mountains, our convincing that you are not who they seek is believable then, as we would not show guilt that we are running."

Ski-be-nan-ted looked into the flames of the fire as he thought about that. He understood Crying Wolf's interpretation. Only someone with something to hide or on the run would risk their life by heading into the swamplands in the middle of winter. He looked over to Crying Wolf who sat crossed legged with his blanket wrapped around his shoulders, warming his hands above the fire.

"We will carry on through the Mountains, I have listened to your reasoning, and I understand your trepidation to stay away from the swamp lands. We are two, those following are three, it is easy to kill that many white men if it is needed."

Crying Wolf looked up and nodded.

"Yes. If it is needed," he replied solemnly.

"For now, we will not worry," Ski-be-nan-ted wrapped his blanket around his shoulders, and the two grew silent as the flames from their fire danced hypnotically to-and-fro.

Chapter 19

It was the evening of the 14th after three days of hard tracking and two cold evenings when Colby finally made contact with the two men he was tracking. They sat huddled around their evening fire content and unaware, or so he thought of his presence. In a silent hush, he commanded Black Dog to 'alert and guard', as he looked on through the bramble. Recognizing who he thought to be Crying Wolf, he stirred in the bushes to get a better view. It only took the sound of one branch snapping to alert the two men, and they looked in the direction from which the sound came.

The only arsenal Colby had with him was the .45 Colt that Crying Wolf himself had given him when they departed way back in Willow Gate. His rifle was still in its scabbard back with his horse. He lay motionless wishing he had been more careful, it was too late though. He had alerted the men of his presence. Silently raising his head, he looked again at the two men. They no longer seemed to be looking his way, and he ever so slowly crawled backwards and deeper into the forest. Standing now he made his way back to his horse, taking him by the reins he led him a short distance away and tethered him.

Removing his rifle, he once more made his way within viewing distance of the two men and their evening fire. This time though he viewed them from the opposite side. He was certain now more than ever that one of the men was indeed Crying Wolf. The other man he couldn't make out. He wondered then if perhaps he hadn't been following Ski-be-nan-ted at all, but rather Crying Wolf and company. It had been at least two years since he had last seen Ski-be-nan-ted up close. What would Crying Wolf be doing way out here? Was the question that burned.

Colby inhaled deeply as he brought his rifle up to his shoulder and sighted in on the men. He always seemed to see better looking with the iron sights of his rifle, his eyes then it seemed, weren't distracted by other things. He conjured up the memory he had of Ski-be-nan-ted and the more he looked and studied him, the more he was convinced he had indeed found him. Why, was he with Crying Wolf, was a question he could not answer.

"That sure looks the Kid who is sitting with Crying Wolf, Black Dog. Leastwise from here," Colby said in a whisper. "Ain't sure why either is in the company of the other. I guess it is like Riley said, the Kid had communications with a friend and they arranged to meet up. Who would've ever thought though, that friend would be Crying Wolf," he added as he continued his gaze of the two.

Tyrell and Riley had managed to get all the particulars worked out with the two dead men, Alvin, and his brother. They sent a wire to the Mounties in Clear Water and were now a day's ride east of Beacon Hill and making their way back to where they had sent Colby off on his own.

"Can't complain too much about the weather, these past couple of days, I will admit though the evening's including this one ain't been to pleasant. We're going to have to stop soon, and make camp."

"I reckon so. By mid-day tomorrow we should be on Colby's trail, and hopefully catch up to him," Riley stated as the two carried on for a few more miles. Finding a spot along the trail, they halted their horses and made their evening camp.

"You want beans and biscuits, Riley?"

"I could eat, yes sir. Sounds fine to me," Riley responded as Tyrell went about getting the things they'd need together. It didn't take long and soon they were mopping up what was left of their beans with the last couple of biscuits. The coffee pot sat near the flames and it burbled and perked as it finished.

Now with coffee in hand, they conversed as the glow from their fire warmed them.

"You think Colby did all right?"

"I figure he's done fine. Ain't been but a couple of days, Black Dog will keep him safe and alert him of anything that might be threatening," Tyrell took a swallow from the cup in his hands, and looked across to Riley.

"I reckon as long as he kept his head screwed on right and didn't go off half cocked he'll be fine."

"I just hope he didn't get lost, the snow was deep when we left him."

"As long as we find his trail, we'll find him. Once we're close, I'm sure Black Dog will let him know that we're near. Don't worry about him."

"I ain't so sure I'm worried, more curious to know how well he managed."

"Well, he ain't stupid. He's a pretty smart fella, I reckon."

"True enough, plus, like you say he's got that dog of yours."

"Yes he does, and Black Dog won't let anything happen to him."

The two of them reminisced until the last of their evening coffee was gone then grabbing their bedrolls they laid them out and closed their eyes. Another evening on the trail had ended.

Colby too was wrapped up in his bedroll a safe distance away from where Crying Wolf and the Kid had made their evening camp. His fire was small and he warmed his hands above the flames as he looked into the coals. A noise in the bush took him off guard and he looked in that direction. Black Dog though didn't flinch and he continued to lie near. It was the dog's undaunted concern that made Colby feel better. He half chuckled as he looked at him.

"You didn't hear that snapping? Shit, sounded like it was over yon some. I figure since you ain't concerned nor will I be," he said as he looked one more time in the direction, to set his mind at ease. He saw nothing and the evening once more became silent except for the crackling of the sticks in his fire.

"I don't suppose we is about to be bushwhacked," he added as he looked again at Black Dog and shrugged. Wrapping his bedroll tighter around his shoulder's he tossed another stick into his fire and made sure that his rifle and his .45 Colt Ranger were both loaded. Then, lying down on the horse blanket he tucked his bedroll in around him and closed his eyes.

Morning came and with it a blue sky and a yellow sun. Crying Wolf and Ski-be-nan-ted were already miles away when Colby and Black Dog were organized enough to head back to where he knew the two of them had camped. He stopped his horse and tethered him as he and Black Dog crept through the bush to where he knew he could see them. To his surprise, the two men were already gone.

"They ain't about no more, dog. Must've headed off before the sun rose, c'mon, let's get back to the horse and get to tracking," he said as he turned and made his way back to his horse. Swinging up onto his saddle he heeled the horses flank and he and Black Dog followed behind.

"Looks like they carried on northerly from here, makes me think they is certainly heading into the Athabasca. That Crying Wolf told us a load of shit, 'bout not wanting anything to do with the Kid. I reckon Travis and Riley are going to be a bit pissed about that," Colby said as much to himself as to the dog and his horse as he carried on.

Tyrell and Riley had risen before the sun to that morning. They were well on their way and getting close to where they'd have to cut north and into the mountains to where they had left Colby and where Alvin and his brother died.

"A couple more hours we should be in the mountains, and following Colby. I don't expect we'll see him though for another day, and that is only if we ride steady," Tyrell said as he looked over to Riley, "how are you doing there Riley, you all right? You've been awful quiet lately, that wound ain't acting up on you none is it?"

"Nope, it ain't, I'm doing okay, getting tired though of this damn trail. Been on it for quite some time, we have been. Yes sir. Can't wait 'til we close the gap enough on the Kid to make a fair judgment if it is he or not."

"I'd certainly agree with that, it is only a matter of time now, I reckon."

The two grew silent for a short while as they continued. Riley finally broke the monotony of their silence.

"We've seen a lot of death again this time 'round too, Travis. First there was the massacre at Cross's place, then finding Gabe Roy's well ate remains. Then we come across Atalmore and his men with no heads on their shoulders nonetheless. We tie a man to a tree who was frozen in the creek, and then Alvin and his brother. Jesus, it plays on a man's mind. I've been thinking on it for quite a while and the more I think on it, the more I find it to be senseless."

"I will admit it don't sit well with me none either. I know though it is all going to end eventually. Besides, today is too nice to be worrying about what we have seen or have been a part of. We have to keep our focus on the job at hand, and with the sun as warm as it is, I think we'll do good today."

Three hours later, they cut off the trail and followed their old slightly melted trail to where Alvin and his brother died. They rested a short distance away and swung off their horses.

"See, told ya we'd do good today. We're following Colby's trail and he's following the Kid and the second rider. All is good Riley," Tyrell took a swig from his canteen. Although it was January it was one of the warmest days that month, and the two basked in the hot sun as they conversed.

"It only makes sense that it is the Kid, we ain't saw no other trail after finding that Appaloosa, and unless the Kid vanished into nothingness, I'd say he is one of the two riders that Colby is following."

"It'd be quite the thing if it weren't, Riley."

"It would mean we lost him, and I ain't so akin to trying to find his trail again. It turns out it ain't him, to hell with it. We'll head back to the Fort. At least we know Atalmore and his men have been found. The Kid will show up somewhere eventually if we don't put cuffs on him this time."

"I reckon if it turns out that way, I ain't going to argue returning to the Fort. You're right if it ain't he whom we've been following, he'll show up somewhere if he don't die in the elements before then, or gets picked up by the law elsewhere."

Colby pulled up to where the trail he was following crested the mountain, the trail now headed southwest and to lower altitudes. He followed at a good pace leaving behind tell tale signs for Tyrell and Riley who he assumed were by now following the same trail. If things had gone as they had expected, then, Colby knew they were closing in and maybe only a day's ride easterly of where he was now. He was glad to be heading off the mountain. It was a bit treacherous as he descended, but finally he made his way. What lay ahead he could see was another wagon road and it along with the men he was following headed southerly. He slowed his horse to a stop and looked in both directions, wondering if the road he was now on was the same road the three of them were following when they lost the Kid. It made sense as he thought about it. The two men he was following had simply chosen to cut across the mountain rather than stay on the main trail, all men on the run did the same.

"Looks like we is now on the damn trail we was on a few days ago," Colby said in a hushed breath. If he remembered correctly and it was the trail they were last on, then he knew it also headed west in the direction of Crab Apple. It was he knew close to the Athabasca territory, it made sense now why he had seen Crying Wolf, and it made sense now that is exactly where the men he was following were heading.

"Shit, we could've stayed on the trail, dog, and we would have crossed their paths here. They is heading southwesterly and into the Athabasca. This road will certainly make for easy tracking now, as long as they stay on it," Colby inhaled deeply. He knew there was a possibility that those he was following may have cut off into the mountains along the way, for now though they were sticking to the road, and he would too.

Keeping up his pace, he managed to gain some distance between himself and the two riders. They were close now, he could sense it, and by dusk that day, he could see two riders ahead. Black Dog had seen them too but he remained at Colby's side. Colby slowed his horse down and looked on. They were far enough away that they hadn't noticed him, or so he thought. He watched in the shadows as the two riders turned a bend in the road and vanished from his sight. He waited a few minutes. Then, he carried on keeping himself hidden, as best he could, along the trail.

"We are being followed closely, by one rider, Crying Wolf," Ski-be-nan-ted said as the two of them continued.

"Yes, one rider does approach. We will stop not far from here, and wait."

"Why would only one be following, when there were three?"

"I cannot be sure. Many white men use these roads. Perhaps we should not worry," Crying Wolf replied. "We will know soon enough once we stop. A single traveler with a destination will pass us by, one following us with intent, will not."

"So, we sit and wait?"

"We sit, we wait, we watch. Yes."

"If it s one of those three men, then what?"

"We will talk."

"Talk, I have no desire to talk to a man who seeks me for monetary gain. I would rather put a knife in his chest, or bullet through his heart."

"We will not act in violence unless it is needed. Those three men as I have told you before are friends. One that rides with them is known by you from distant years gone by, his name is Colby Christian, you and he have been in the presence of each other in the past."

"I have not heard that name in many years. Yes, I know of Colby Christian. How can he be a man of law?"

"Time changes people. You too have changed Ski-be-nan-ted. Everyone changes."

"Yes, people change, hate though does not. The white man has hated me for many years."

"It is because they do not know the whole truth. They are commanded by the white man's laws. All that they know about you is what they have been told and heard tale of. They do not know the truth as seen from your eyes."

"They have never given me the chance. I was guilty of all that has been told about me to them from the beginning. They do not care about the truth. Those you call your friends that track me cannot be any different."

"Those three men are different, Ski-be-nan-ted. I have sat many times with them around evening fires, have bedded down in their evening camps, and brought back to health in their houses. They are not like the white men from years gone past. They see things not only from their points of view, but also from the points of view of all races and creeds. They are fair men."

"If those men are anything like that, then why must I run from their ropes and bars?"

"You already have the answer, Ski-be-nan-ted. It is because those that accused you of those things influenced those that believed. I did not say all white men are fair, I said the three tracking you are fair and just men. That is why we will not raise our arms in violence if the one that alone now follows, is one of those three men. Nor will we raise our arms in violence if the man that follows is a simple passer-by," Crying Wolf slowed his horse down, "tonight, we will stay here," he said as the two of them swung off their horses and tethered them.

It took a few minutes to gather enough dry wood to keep their fire going throughout the night, and to set up their camp. With the task finished, they sat crossed legged on their horse blankets around the flickering flames and waited to see if whoever it was, that was following them caught up. No one did. They knew then that it was indeed one of the three men that had been tracking, Ski-be-nan-ted.

"It is true then, the man following is one of your three friends that have tracked me, because no man has yet caught up. A single traveler with no intent would have by now passed us by."

Crying Wolf nodded.

"Yes. It is either, Travis, Riley, or Colby. I do not know why either is alone," Crying Wolf stood up. "I we will go meet them..." he began as he heard the audible click of a pistol being cocked. Colby, who had circled around along with Black Dog now stood in the shadows.

"Nope, you ain't going anywhere Crying Wolf," Colby looked toward the fire, "and you Ski-be-nan-ted, don't even try going for that Hawken." Colby stepped out of the shadows in view of each of them. "I've been following the two of you for a few days, already," he gently released the hammer of his pistol and slapped it back into its holster.

"See, I told you, that one day you would not have a use for a long gun," Crying Wolf said.

"I ain't sure how to respond to that at the moment. I'm trying to figure out what it is I'm looking at. Goddamn it, Ski-be-nan-ted, it has been a long time," Colby looked on and shook his head. He wished now that who he looked at wasn't Ski-be-nan-ted, but it was. It was up to him alone he knew, to make the arrest. Colby though hadn't changed his mind from when he, Riley and Tyrell were in Nowhere and they had heard tale of the Shepherd. From that day on it made no sense to him whatsoever that Ski-be-nan-ted, deserved to be apprehended. Especially since, he knew what the outcome to that would likely be. Ski-be-nan-ted had certainly, not been treated fairly by the laws that had accused him.

It was one of the reasons he insisted he follow alone, while, Tyrell and Riley headed back to Beacon Hill, with Alvin and his brother. He knew if he came upon Ski-be-nan-ted before they returned, he'd simply tell them that it wasn't the Kid after all that they had been tracking. He would simply let him go.

"Many seasons have come and gone. Many seasons ago, you sat with me among mutual friends, they were not lawful men, yet today you stand before me, as a lawman of sorts. How has your life been Colby?"

"A lot has changed Ski-be-nan-ted. I met some good men, shot many bad men, and today I find you among the living. Many stories of your death have been wide spread. I think it is best that you stay dead."

"What is this you say? Are you going to kill me?"

"No sir, I haven't seen you," Colby smiled as he knelt next to their fire and warmed his hands.

"You do not wish to take me in?"

"Nope, I sure don't. You are in the company of Crying Wolf, and we know him to be good. I'll tell the others, that it wasn't you we've been trailing."

"Will they believe this?"

"I don't reckon they'll much care. The old fella Riley, I think simply wants to return to the Fort, and Travis, well I think if it were him sitting here, he'd cuff you and bring you in. I ain't so sure that be best. I know you have kept some cattlemen free of cattle rustling and have put to death some of those cattle rustlers. They call you the Shepherd, a man who has protected their livelihoods. You have done more good than bad, I think."

"I have been accused of many things of which I did not do, but, yes, I have killed many bad men though. But, I am not the savage killer the white man has made me out to be."

The three men grew silent for a moment as they contemplated.

"You can tell the others, that it was me you found, and that I was in the company of the Apache Warrior, Three Wolves Running," Crying Wolf suggested.

"Three Wolves Running, and who is he?"

"He was our brother, the brother that Gabe Roy killed."

Colby was shocked to hear this.

"You and Ski-be-nan-ted are brothers?"

"Yes. He was taken from our home at a very young age, many years ago, and adopted by a white man. When the Indian wars ended, he left to fight with the white man, to this day, I still do not know why. The Athabasca accepted that as his wish to do good things, and we waited for his return. Years of deceit and lies told by the white man kept him away from his home. I had a vision on where I would find him, and I did. Now I bring him home to the family that has missed him," Crying Wolf looked into the flames of the fire.

Colby looked over to Ski-be-nan-ted and smiled.

"It is with pleasure that I have met you Three Wolves Running. It is the name I will use when I tell the others who it is that I found on this night. That you ain't who we thought you was, but are the Apache Warrior, Three Wolves Running."

"I will forever be grateful for that my friend Colby."

"You must promise me, that when I leave here, that you two will carry on to the Athabasca territory. I think there you will be safe from those that still look for the Apache Kid. I will not reveal your identity, as I know what fate likely waits for you. Stay with Crying Wolf and live the rest of your life within the laws that govern this land."

"How will you convince the others that it is not I that you have been tracking?"

"I don't think it'll take much to convince them. They ain't here to see that it is you," Colby shrugged. "I will be convincing."

"Will you join us now for tea?" Crying Wolf asked.

"I wouldn't turn down a hot drink. Thank you, Crying Wolf. Yes, I'll drink tea with you."

Crying Wolf poured him a cup and handed it to him.

"It has been a long time since I have drunk sweet tea," Colby said as he took it from him and warmed his hands around the tin cup.

"I have to wonder, where are Travis and Riley?"

"There was an incident a few nights ago, that entailed them to bring two dead men back to civilization. They headed back to Beacon Hill, have likely been heading back this way for a day or so."

"Two dead men, what happened to these men?"

Colby told the story.

"So, Atalmore and the others are dead?"

"Yes sir. Their heads were taken, clean off their shoulders. At first, we thought it was the Apache Kid, that did the slaughtering, but turns out it wasn't. We do know you was with them at one time or the other."

"I was indeed with them for three days ride; they were heading back the way I was fleeing from. We parted ways."

"That is what we conjured, after we came across the man who claimed his brother Alvin did the killings. Then, we found your trail and the horse you were seen riding. Your first mistake was taking a branded horse," Colby took a slurp from the cup in his hand.

"There will be no need for me to steal horses anymore. Soon, I will be home."

"Yes, soon we will be home Ski-be-nan-ted, soon you will be back where you belong. The Athabasca will forever be in your debt, young Colby. You have seen things in a different light then what others may see."

"It is only because of the company Ski-be-nan-ted is in, that I will turn my head and say it is not he who we have been tracking. Back at Willow Gate, you were part of the onslaught that brought justice to Gabe Roy. The two or three men you brought down with arrows may have killed any of us, but we all survived those attacks and the final battle due to your presence. It is another reason why I will turn my head and let Ski-be-nan-ted go. I ain't able to justify in my mind bringing him in."

A quarter mile away and gaining distance was Tyrell and Riley, they had decided to follow Colby's trail even as the darkness of evening approached. The snow and moon light helped guide them and now they could see in the distance the small fire that burned, where Colby, Crying Wolf, and Ski-be-nan-ted congregated. The two men slowed their horses to a stop.

"I'd say that is our destination," Riley said as the two of them looked on.

"I reckon. C'mon, let's get." Tyrell said as the two of them continued. It didn't take long before Black Dog sat up and looked back.

"Something is coming our way," Colby said as the three of them looked in the direction.

"Yes, two men on horses. Perhaps, my freedom will be short lived."

"If it is Travis and Riley, we'll introduce you as Three Wolves Running. I ain't sure how convincing we'll be, but I know we ain't got a picture of you Ski-be-nan-ted. Their only memory of you is what is in their minds. You might consider hiding that Hawken by your side. What we do know is that the Apache Kid uses one," Colby stood up and looked on as Ski-be-nan-ted hid the Hawken out of view.

Black Dog now pranced forward a telltale sign that it was indeed Tyrell and Riley approaching.

"I'd say that is Travis and Riley, put on your poker faces," Colby said as the three of them waited for the confrontation.

A few minutes later, the two men pulled up to the fire, shocked to see Crying Wolf and another along with Colby, nonchalantly waiting for their approach.

"Crying Wolf? What the hell?"

"Hello, Travis. Please, come. Sit by our fire. The two of you must be weary from your travels. Colby tells me the tale on why we have met like this. You have been seeking Ski-be-nan-ted, but have been fooled by him."

"Who is that you got with you there, Crying Wolf?" Riley was quick to question as the two swung off their horses.

"I am Three Wolves Running, and you must be the old codger Colby calls Riley, and the other with you is Travis-both friends I'm told of the Athabasca," Ski-be-nan-said as he stood up and approached the two with his hand outstretched. His entire demeanor changed, he had become the Apache Warrior. His facial express and body language all changed from who he was only a few minutes earlier, and he looked nothing like Ski-be-nan-ted. Colby noted this change, and it spooked him some, he couldn't understand how or why and now he really didn't care. If it helped convince the others, then so be it. Only Ski-be-nan-ted and Crying Wolf understood the reasons why. Their brother the Apache Warrior, Three Wolves Running, had made good the promise in Crying Wolf's vision to protect Ski-be-nan-ted, and his spirit now possessed him. Ski-be-nan-ted had become Three Wolves Running.

Both Tyrell and Riley stepped forward and shook the man's hand, neither was completely convinced, but Colby managed to put their mind at ease, and they saw no .50 caliber Hawken.

"It is like Crying Wolf says it is. We must've lost the Kid's trail, and been following Crying Wolf and Three Wolves Running. We've been waiting here for you two most of the day. I knew you was close, and I thought it be best that yous see for yourselves who it is we've been trailing. Rather than me heading back to let yous know. This here least wise you can see for yourselves that we ain't been tracking the Kid," Colby fibbed.

"Well, Goddamn," Tyrell said as he crouched and warmed his hands above the flames, he looked over to Crying Wolf and squinted from the smoke that blew into his eyes. He wondered at that moment if it was as Colby had said. It could be exactly like that he knew, it might not be too. He averted his eyes to Three Wolves Running and as far as he could tell from memory, the man didn't look anything like how he remembered the Kid to look like. He had seen black and white sketches and photos of him in newsprint and such over the years, and although he knew, time changed how people looked, he was convinced enough to accept the fact that who he was looking at wasn't the Kid.

"I have to tell you, it seems damn odd to see you way out here, Crying Wolf," Riley began as he too now crouched and warmed his own hands above the flickering flames.

"It is as likely odd for you as it is for me, to see you three. Our reasons for being here though, I know are much different. From what Colby talks about, I can understand your concerns. As I told you as we parted ways in Willow Gate, the squared jaw Apache, Ski-be-nan-ted, will not be protected by the Athabasca. Before the big winter storm came, us two were returning from a wake of an elder Algonquin, that too I'm sure seems odd. But, it is truth," Crying Wolf convinced. "We were returning to the Athabasca, and were in the mountains when the storm came, it is where you three happened upon our trail through the snow, and it is because of that, we sit here now in the company of each other. Had the storm not come, perhaps we wouldn't be so lucky," Crying Wolf smiled.

Tyrell and Riley couldn't dispute the tale and so they simply accepted the fact, that they had lost Ski-be-nan-ted.

"Are we going to keep tracking the Kid or what?" Colby questioned, as much to bring attention to Crying Wolf's tale and to avert attention away from Three Wolves Running.

"Shit, I don't know. What do you think Riley?"

"As I told yous before, if who we've been tracking ain't who we assumed them to be, which, it seems clear to me it ain't, then I say to hell with it. I'm tired of the snow and cold. We is about twenty miles or better from where we lost the Kid's trail. The road we're on now heads east and toward the Fort as far as I can tell. I say we call this one a draw. The Kid outsmarted us, or for all we know may have been killed by that Alvin fella," Riley responded even though he wasn't convinced of that. His instincts told him he was already in the presence of Ski-be-nan-ted. Yet, he no longer cared.

"So, we head back to the Fort then, and call this one a draw. I do agree with you Riley, I'm tired of this too."

"We're just going to give up like that?" Colby questioned to add more deception to what was, and, what wasn't.

"Twenty miles Colby is a lot, three days ride back the way we've come, that'd put the Kid at least six days ahead, in whichever direction he may have headed. Nope, this one is a loss."

"I never thought the two of you would give up so damn easily, but, I ain't in charge, so I guess we do it your way," Colby shook his head as though to show his disagreement, although he was relieved.

There were a few minutes of awkward silence. Finally, Crying Wolf spoke.

"Tonight I invite you to our fire, spend it here with us, we have food, warmth of fire, and friendship. Weariness and hunger battles all men in times of snow and cold. It will also battle with the one you seek. I think he will be dead before he finds warmth and friendship."

Crying Wolf it seemed was sincere and he was right, the Kid would die in the elements if he didn't find sanctuary soon.

"Thank you for the invite Crying Wolf and we'll certainly take you up on that offer."

"Good it is settled then, let us sit as friends, and enjoy food, warmth, and conversation."

Sometime later, the howling of wolves in the distance singled the time of night, and the five men laid out their bedrolls, stoked their fire, and closed their eyes.

In the early predawn of January 16, Crying Wolf and Ski-be-nan-ted slipped into the forest and headed for home, leaving behind one single purple-feathered arrow. It was Colby, who had found it. He looked in the direction the two men headed, and smiled.

"Stay on the right side of things, Ski-be-nan-ted, or it is my ass," he said in a hushed voice as he returned to the fire and stoked it. Tyrell and Riley slowly came to life as he poured his first coffee of the day. Again, it was a warm morning and the sun was slowly creeping into view.

"They is gone already," Riley stated as he stood up and yawned.

"Was gone long before I rose, I reckon. Crying Wolf left behind an arrow," Colby said as he took a slurp of his morning coffee.

"A good sign that is," Riley made his way over to the fire and poured his own coffee. He crouched and looked around he was glad they'd be heading east and not back the way they came, still in search of the Kid, whom he assumed had rode away that morning with Crying Wolf. It mattered little, some things in life he knew were better left alone than picked at, and sometime's in life it was better to look the other way, and that is what he'd do now.

Tyrell rose next and relieved himself before making his way over to the fire.

"Morning Riley, Colby," he said as he nodded at them. Pouring himself a coffee, he noticed the arrow and he gestured with his chin toward it, "that's always a good sign ain't it?"

"Is too, yes indeed," Riley said with a smile, for one reason or the other that morning he felt better than he had in past mornings. Even Colby and Tyrell seemed to be in better spirits than they had been in the past since taking on the task that had brought them to where they were now, although an unfinished task, they were glad it was over for now. Soon they'd be back at the Fort and some normalcy.

Chapter 20

On January 23, the three of them pulled their horses up to the McCoy's corral and unloaded their gear. Tired, hungry and weather beaten they entered the office from the back door and were greeted by Ed, Brady and Tanner. Tanner had made some head way with Emery Nelson's murder and had returned to the Fort four days earlier.

"Welcome home, men," Ed said as he leaned up against the front counter.

"It is good to be back, I'll tell yous that," Riley responded as he sat down on a chair.

"I reckon it would be. You have been gone for quite some time. We got your last wire regarding the Kid. So he fooled yous eh?"

"We was close Ed, had him in view a couple of times, but, like a ghost folks claim him to be he vanished. Disappeared completely. we never found his trail after bringing Alvin and his brother to Beacon Hill."

"That was another damn tragedy wasn't it?"

"It was a damn mess is what it was," Colby said as he looked around.

"It is good to have you with us Colby. Should we make it official today?"

"I'd rather get some rest and food in me before I go through all the, this, that and the other thing."

"I suppose you are all in need of that. McCoy's will flip the bill for steak and whisky at day's end," Ed looked over to Tyrell who hadn't said much. "Travis, you feel all right?"

"I feel fine, Ed, jus' tired and trail sore. I've been gone a long time, it is nice to be home," Tyrell looked at Tanner.

"Sure good to see you Tanner, wasn't expecting you'd be here. How did things go up north in Hazelton?"

"I was able to pin the murder of Emery on that Pinkerton fella, Ranthorp, which, Crawford shot. Seems he assumed Emery was cheating at cards, and decided to steal back the money Emery won from him, five thousand hard cash dollars. Was also able to have the young Constable you and Buck spoke to removed from duty. He was as dirty as the muddy streets of Hazelton."

"So we was right all along, about Ranthorp being the killer?"

"We were, yep."

"I'd say Ranthorp got what was coming to him, and I guess that proves Matt ain't the killer, like some thought."

"The only one who was pushing that ideology was that young Constable, who has now been stripped of his red tunic and badge," Brady said as he now spoke.

"It is hard to believe the corruption of some that Canada calls their finest, from Willow Gate to Hazelton."

"That is why there is McCoy's," Ed said with a smile. He was proud of each man that worked for him. They were the best there was no doubt about it.

"I'd like to sit and idly chat with you all, but, I need rest a bath and food. Do any of you know if the widow Donale has any rooms for rent?" Colby asked in exhaustion.

"You can bunk with me, Colby. The upstairs apartment is big enough," Tyrell offered.

"No offense Travis, but, I've been in the company of you and Riley for a long-time now, and would like to have my own damn place to sleep."

"I'm sure the widow has a boarding room, Colby. McCoy's will even pay for the first month."

"That is kind of you Ed, and thank you. I'll gather my things and head over there now. I'll see all of yous in the morning."

"You ain't going to join us for steak and whisky tonight?"

"I'll likely still be sleeping. I've been kept awake by Riley's snoring for the past few weeks. Nope, I'll pass on the steak."

"All right, hang on I have your pay and I'll pay for a month's rental at the widows," Ed said as he turned and made his way to the McCoy's cash fund. He handed Colby two hundred dollars for his pay, and another fifty for his rental at the widows. "There, that ought to cover your rent and pay for the work you have helped with. Come morning we're going to have to make things official, and we'll get you on a regular pay."

Colby took the money, thanked him, and headed off to seek himself a room at the widow Donale's place. It wasn't long afterwards that Tyrell and Riley did the same and headed to their own places.

On January 24, at the morning meeting after Colby Christian became a full-fledged employee of McCoy's, Ed announced his retirement to the crew.

"I have been at this job for forty years. I started back when I was a twenty-one year old kid. I'm pushing sixty-two and have had a great life, have a decent savings and a wonderful wife, and my son, Brady, he ain't so bad either," Ed chuckled.

"So, on this day I announce to all of you including our newest employee Colby, that at the end of January I won't be coming into the office. Brady will take over from there on. I'm pleased as I can be about the men working here. I trust each of you and know you are all damn fine men. Brady will grow the operation however, he sees fit. I'll come by every now and again to make sure he's walking the line. But, my bounty hunting days have come and gone, and with the way things are changing in this industry it is time to let the younger and fit roll with the punches, and new approaches," Ed looked at each of them and smiled.

"Goddamn it, Ed, you can't retire. I'm as old as you if not a couple years your senior. If you retire where does that leave me?" Riley was distraught, "maybe I ought to consider retirement myself."

"I knew you were going to feel that way, Riley, and I can't make up your mind for you. In all honesty I do believe Brady was going to make you a senior investigator, it comes with a wage increase and more time in the office than out on the trail."

"Wage increase and more time in the office, doesn't sound like me, Ed, no sir," Riley shook his head as he contemplated.

"Shit, c'mon Riley. You're needed here."

"I don't know, Brady. A senior investigator don't mean much to an old folk like me. I have been in this business for a long time too, was even shot again this last trip," Riley pulled up his shirt and showed the scar. "We didn't even find out who the hell it was that shot me. It ruined my best shirt and everything."

"We never knew you took a piece of lead."

"It was all healed up by the time we made it back. There weren't no point in bringing it up yesterday. I bring it up today, 'cause I'm still pissed about it, and with Ed retiring it gets my mind whirling maybe it is best that I do the same. The next bullet might kill me."

"Well, I ain't retiring Riley for another week. So, you have time to decide and think about it."

"And whatever it is you decide Riley, we'll respect."

"I've already decided. This is the only job I have ever done and the only job I like. I ain't going to be stuck in the damn office though. I tell ya's that. I will take a wage increase though," Riley chuckled. "For a moment there I was thinking I might run cattle on my homestead, but, that switch turned off quick when I thought on it. I'll stick around for a while longer I reckon. It isn't going to be the same though, without you Ed."

"I'll still make myself present, and do a lil' bit here and there, but, it'll be Brady that signs off on your pays."

On January 31 1892, Ed McCoy retired from the business he had built from the ground up with his own blood, sweat, and eagerness to keep the bad guys in check. Riley became the senior investigator and took over Brady McCoy's duties while Brady took over Ed's. The others, Tyrell Sloan *aka* Travis Sweet, Tanner McBride, Colby Christian, and Matt Crawford remained on the McCoy's payroll and the business continued. Their motto to this day remains as it were. *"If you can't find them, we will."*

www.ingramcontent.com/pod-product-compliance
Lightning Source LLC
Chambersburg PA
CBHW061257210726
48293CB00003B/1004